Wishbone™ Classics

THE ADVENTURES of TOM SAWYER

by Mark Twain

adapted by Stephen Fuentes

Interior illustrations by Joe Boddy

Wishbone illustrations by Kathryn Yingling

S0-AQJ-433

HarperPaperbacks

A Division of HarperCollins*Publishers*

This is a work of fiction. The characters, incidents, and dialogues are products of the author's imagination and are not to be construed as real. Any resemblance to actual events or persons, living or dead, is entirely coincidental.

HarperPaperbacks *A Division of* HarperCollins*Publishers*
10 East 53rd Street, New York, N.Y. 10022

Copyright ©1997 Big Feats! Entertainment
All rights reserved. No part of this book may be used or reproduced in any manner whatsoever without written permission of the publisher, except in the case of brief quotations embodied in critical articles and reviews. For information address HarperCollins*Publishers*, 10 East 53rd Street, New York, N.Y. 10022.

Cover photographs by Carol Kaelson

A Creative Media Applications Production
Art Direction by Fabia Wargin Design

First printing: January 1997

Printed in the United States of America

HarperPaperbacks and colophon are trademarks of HarperCollins*Publishers*
WISHBONE is a trademark and service mark of Big Feats! Entertainment

❖ 10 9 8 7

TOM SAWYER

Introduction

All set to enter a world of action, adventure, drama, and
laughs? Then come along with me, **Wishbone**. You may
have seen me on my TV show. Often I am the main
character and sometimes I am the sidekick, but I'm
always right in the middle of a thrilling story. Now, I'm
going to be your guide as we explore one of the world's
greatest books — THE ADVENTURES OF TOM SAWYER.
Together we'll meet a lot of interesting characters and
discover places we've never been! I guarantee lots of
surprises too! So find a nice comfy chair, and get ready
to read with **Wishbone**.

Table of Contents

ABOUT THE AUTHOR

Let me introduce you to one of the greatest American authors–Samuel Langhorne Clemens. You may know him by his famous pen name, Mark Twain.

Mark Twain's book THE ADVENTURES OF TOM SAWYER tells the story of a young boy and his exciting adventures along the Mississippi River. Twain knew all about these adventures firsthand. He grew up on the banks of the wide Mississippi, and his greatest memories were of his adventures on the river.

Samuel Clemens was born in the town of Florida, Missouri, on November 30, 1835. Halley's comet, which can be seen only once approximately every 75 years, flamed in the sky the night he was born.

Sam's family moved to Hannibal, Missouri, when he was four years old. Hannibal was on the banks of the Mississippi, and Sam grew up in the shadow of the majestic river. The river carried steamboats, rafts, and many other kinds of boats through Hannibal, down to St. Louis, on to New Orleans, and into the Gulf of Mexico. The river was crowded with boats and tradesmen, and Sam was able to see people from all over the world as the Mississippi rolled by his hometown.

Sam's father died when he was 12, and Sam had to go to work as an apprentice printer. One of his jobs was setting the type for the printing press, and Sam learned a lot about history and literature by reading the books and articles he was printing.

When he was young, Sam dreamed of being a riverboat pilot. In his book about the river, *Life on the Mississippi*, he wrote: "When I was a boy, there was but one permanent ambition among my comrades in our village on the west bank of the Mississippi River. That was to be a steamboatman." At the age of twenty-two, Sam fulfilled his dream of working on the river when he became a licensed steamboat pilot.

When he became a writer, Sam selected a pen name. Often a writer uses a pen name to hide his or her identity, but Sam also used his pen name to pay tribute to the Mississippi River. Sam's pen name—Mark Twain—is a phrase he often heard echoing across the great river. Riverboat pilots used the phrase "mark twain" to measure distance. The call meant the river was two fathoms (about twelve feet) deep, and the water was safe for the riverboat.

Mark Twain wrote many books, including *The Adventures of Huckleberry Finn, The Prince and the Pauper*, and *Personal Recollections of Joan of Arc*. But *The Adventures of Tom Sawyer* was special because it was based on his childhood. Writing *The Adventures of Tom Sawyer* was Mark Twain's way of paying tribute to his boyhood experiences.

Mark Twain died on April 21, 1910, the year that Halley's comet made another appearance in the sky. Twain's books have been read and enjoyed by millions of people, and he is celebrated as one of the greatest American writers.

ABOUT THE ADVENTURES OF TOM SAWYER

The **WISHBONE** *classics* version of *The Adventures of Tom Sawyer* is called an adaptation because Mark Twain's original book was abridged and adapted to create this version. First the original book was abridged, which means scenes were cut to make the book shorter. Then the book was adapted, which means certain words from the original book were changed to make them more accessible to a modern reader. To remain true to the spirit of the original book, most of Mark Twain's language, style, spelling, and even punctuation was left unchanged in this **WISHBONE** *classics* version.

I think you're really going to like my version of THE ADVENTURES OF TOM SAWYER. Check out the original version, too!

The characters in the book talk as they did in Mark Twain's hometown of Hannibal a long, long time ago. For example, in the book Huckleberry Finn says: "A body can't be too partic'lar how they talk 'bout these-yer dead people, Tom." This style might take a little getting used to at first, but when you think about it, it is easy to understand what Huck is really saying: "People can't be too particular about how they talk about these dead people, Tom."

Mark Twain had a special gift for writing the way boys and girls just like you really talked over 100 years ago!

There may be some other words in this book that you don't understand. That's why there is a glossary, or a "mini-dictionary," at the back of the book. Some of the more difficult words are defined for you in the glossary.

I always sniff around the glossary when I don't know what a word means!

Because he was writing so long ago, Mark Twain refers to some people using words that are not appropriate to use now. For example, one of the characters in the book is called "Injun" Joe. Although a term like this may have been acceptable in Mark Twain's times, it is not used anymore because it is considered insulting. As with all books, the word choices used by the writer should be considered in relation to the time in which the book was written.

MAIN CHARACTERS

Tom Sawyer — the star of our story
Huckleberry Finn — Tom's friend
Joe Harper — Tom's friend
Becky Thatcher — a girl in Tom's class
Aunt Polly — Tom's aunt and guardian
Sid — Tom's younger half-brother.
Mary — Tom's kind-hearted cousin
Injun Joe — an evil man

SETTING

*T*he *Adventures of Tom Sawyer* takes place in St. Petersburg, Missouri, on the banks of the Mississippi River. Tom's adventures in St. Petersburg were inspired by events that really happened in Hannibal, Missouri, where Mark Twain grew up. In the preface to Twain's original book, he writes: "Most of the adventures recorded in this book really occurred; one or two were experiences of my own, the rest those of boys who were schoolmates of mine." Many of the places you will read about in this book actually existed in Hannibal; one example is McDowell's cave, which is called McDougal's cave in the book.

The Adventures of Tom Sawyer takes place in the period before the Civil War, more than 100 years ago! Mark Twain's book is true to the setting, or the time period and location, of the story. So *The Adventures of Tom Sawyer* is not just a great story; it is also an accurate look at how people lived in this time and place.

Mark Twain included many odd superstitions in the book. These superstitions were commonly believed during the time period of this story. In one adventure, Tom Sawyer and Huck Finn take a dead cat to the graveyard at midnight because they *believe* this will cure warts. In his adventure on Jackson's Island Tom won't swim because the rattlesnake rattles he wore around his ankle were gone and he *believed* he would have cramps without this "mysterious charm." It may not seem logical, but Tom and his friends really believe these superstitions.

OK, I'm ready! Let's jump in and join Tom on his adventures!

1
Y-o-u-u Tom

"Tom!"

No answer.

"Tom!"

No answer.

"What's gone with that boy, I wonder? You TOM!"

No answer.

The old lady pulled her eyeglasses down and looked over them about the room; then she put them up and looked out under them. She seldom or never looked *through* them for so small a thing as a boy; they were her state pair, the pride of her heart, and were built for "style," not service—she could have seen through a pair of stove lids just as well. She looked puzzled for a moment, and then said, not fiercely, but still loud enough for the furniture to hear:

"Well, I lay if I get hold of you I'll—"

She did not finish, for by this time she was bending down and punching under the bed with the broom. She resurrected nothing but the cat.

"I never did see the beat of that boy!"

She went to the open door and stood in it and looked out among the tomato vines and "jimpson" weeds that made up the garden. No Tom. **Jimpson or jimson weeds are**

poisonous plants. Not the sort of thing you want growing in your garden! So she lifted up her voice and shouted:

"Y-o-u-u *Tom*!"

There was a slight noise behind her and she turned just in time to grab a small boy by the slack of his jacket and arrest his flight.

"There! I might 'a' thought of that closet. What you been doing in there?"

"Nothing."

"Nothing! Look at your hands. And look at your mouth. What is that?

"*I* don't know, aunt."

"Well, *I* know. It's jam—that's what it is. Forty times I've said if you didn't let that jam alone I'd skin you. Hand me that switch."

A switch is a thin stick used for whipping. Nowadays, we call it spanking. When Mark Twain was a boy, a whipping was what kids got when they got into trouble.

The switch hovered in the air—the peril was desperate.

"My! Look behind you, aunt!"

The old lady whirled round, and snatched her skirts out of danger. The lad fled on the instant, scrambled up the high board-fence, and disappeared over it.

His Aunt Polly stood surprised a moment, and then broke into a gentle laugh.

"Hang the boy, can't I never learn anything? Ain't he played me tricks enough like that for me to be looking out for him by this time? But old fools is the biggest fools there is. Can't learn an old dog new tricks, as the saying is. **Hey, wait a minute! A dog can learn a new trick anytime — sometimes we just don't want to.** He's my own dead sister's boy, poor thing, and I ain't got the heart to lash him, somehow. Every time I let him off, my conscience does hurt me so, and every time I hit him my old heart almost breaks. He'll play hookey this evening, and I'll just be obleeged to make him work tomorrow, to punish him. It's mighty hard to make him work Saturdays, when all the boys is having holiday, but he hates work more than he hates anything else, and I've *got* to do some of my duty by him."

Tom did play hookey, and he had a very good time.

That Tom is quite a trickster. He fooled his Aunt Polly to get out of a whipping, and then he played hookey. (That means he skipped school.) But Aunt Polly is pretty clever, too, and she knows something that Tom hates even more than a whipping. What will Tom's punishment be? Keep reading to find out!

2
Strategic Movements

When you're a kid—or a dog—there are only three rules on Saturday: play, have lots of fun, and play some more. But not for Tom. Today is his punishment for skipping school. And what could be worse than one of Aunt Polly's whippings? Why, work, of course—and on Saturday, too! On the biggest play day of the week, Tom is being made to whitewash—that means paint— Aunt Polly's fence.

Tom appeared on the sidewalk with a bucket of whitewash and a long-handled brush. He looked over the fence, and all gladness left him, and a deep sadness settled down upon his spirit. Thirty yards of board fence nine feet high. Life to him seemed hollow, and existence but a burden. Sighing, he dipped his brush and passed it along the topmost plank; repeated the operation; did it again; and sat down on a tree-box discouraged.

He began to think of the fun he had planned for this day, and his sorrows multiplied. He got out his worldly wealth and examined it—bits of toys, marbles, and trash; enough to buy an exchange of *work*, maybe, but not half enough to buy so much as half an hour of pure freedom. **In Tom's day, kids traded stuff all the time. Their "worldly wealth" was whatever they carried around to trade. Tom was hoping that somebody might do his work for him if he had something really**

good to trade. But, alas, he doesn't. Looks like he'll be stuck whitewashing the fence all day! So he gave up the idea of trying to buy the boys. At this dark and hopeless moment an inspiration burst upon him! Nothing less than a great inspiration.

He took up his brush and went calmly to work. Ben Rogers came into view presently—the very boy, of all boys, whose ridicule he had been dreading. Ben's walk was the hop-skip-and-jump—proof enough that his heart was light. He was eating an apple, and giving a long, melodious whoop, followed by a deep-toned ding-dong-dong, ding-dong-dong, for he was personating a steamboat. As he drew near, he slowed down, took the middle of the street, and leaned far over to starboard—for he was personating the "Big Missouri," and considered himself to be drawing nine feet of water. **Have you ever pretended to be something or somebody else? I'll tell you a secret: I do it all the time! Tom's friend Ben is pretending he is the famous steamboat, the "Big Missouri." On a boat, the right side is the stabboard or starboard, and the left side is the labboard or larboard.** He was boat, and captain, and engine bells combined, so he had to imagine himself standing on his own hurricane-deck giving the orders and executing them:

"Stop her, sir! Ting-a-ling-ling!"

"Ship up to back! Ting-a-ling-ling!"

It sounds like Tom has thought of a great plan to get out of whitewashing the fence!

18

Tom went on whitewashing—paid no attention to the steamboat. Ben stared a moment and then said:

"Hi-*yi*! *You're* up a stump, ain't you!"

No answer. Tom looked over his last touch with the eye of an artist; then he gave his brush another gentle sweep and surveyed the result, as before. Ben ranged up along-side of him. Tom's mouth watered for the apple, but he stuck to his work.

Ben said:

"Hello, old chap, you got to work, hey?"

Tom wheeled suddenly and said:

"Why it's you, Ben! I warn't noticing."

"Say—*I'm* going in a swimming, *I* am. Don't you wish you could? But of course you'd druther *work*—wouldn't you? Course you would!"

Tom studied the boy a bit, and said:

"What do you call work?"

"Why, ain't *that* work?"

Tom resumed his whitewashing, and answered carelessly:

"Well, maybe it is, and maybe it ain't. All I know is, it suits Tom Sawyer."

"Oh, come, now, you don't mean to let on that you *like* it?"

The brush continued to move.

"Like it? Well, I don't see why I oughtn't to like it. Does a boy get a chance to whitewash a fence every day?" **If I'm not mistaken, Tom is up to his trickery again. He's trying to convince Ben that it's more fun to paint Aunt Polly's fence than to go swimming. But wait a minute! Surely Ben won't fall for that . . . will he?**

That put the thing in a new light. Ben stopped

nibbling his apple. Tom swept his brush daintily back and forth—stepped back to note the effect—added a touch here and there—criticised the effect again—Ben watching every move and getting more and more interested, more and more absorbed.

Presently he said:

"Say, Tom, let *me* whitewash a little."

Tom considered, was about to consent; but he changed his mind:

"No-no-I reckon it wouldn't hardly do, Ben. You see, Aunt Polly's awful particular about this fence—right here on the street, you know—but if it was the back fence I wouldn't mind and she wouldn't. Yes, she's awful particular about this fence; it's got to be done very careful; I reckon there ain't one boy in a thousand, maybe two thousand, that can do it the way it's got to be done."

"No—is that so? Oh come, now—lemme just try. Only just a little—I'd let *you*, if you was me, Tom."

"Ben, I'd like to, honest injun; but Aunt Polly—Sid wanted to do it, and she wouldn't let Sid. Now don't you see how I'm fixed? If you was to tackle this fence and anything was to happen to it—" **By the way, Sid is Tom's younger brother. He's kind of a tattletale, and he's almost always the first one to tell Aunt Polly whenever Tom does something wrong.**

"Oh, shucks, I'll be just as careful. Now lemme try. Say—I'll give you the core of my apple."

"Well, here—No, Ben, now don't. I'm afeard—"

"I'll give you *all* of it!"

Tom gave up the brush with reluctance in his face but eagerness in his heart. And while the late steamer "Big Missouri" worked and sweated in the sun, the retired artist sat on a barrel in the shade close by, dangled his legs, munched his apple, and planned the slaughter of more innocents. There was no lack of material; boys happened along every little while; they came to jeer, but remained to whitewash. By the time Ben was tired out, Tom had traded the next chance to Billy Fisher for a kite, in good repair; and when *he* played out, Johnny Miller bought in for a dead rat and a string to swing it with—and so on, and so on, hour after hour. And when the middle of the afternoon came, from being a poor poverty-stricken boy in the morning, Tom was literally rolling in wealth. He had beside the things before mentioned, twelve marbles, part of a jews-harp, a piece of blue bottle-glass to look through, a spool cannon, a key that wouldn't unlock anything, a fragment of chalk, a glass stopper of a decanter, a tin soldier, a couple of tadpoles, six fire-crackers, a kitten with only one eye, a brass door-knob, a dog-collar—but no dog—the handle of a knife, four pieces of orange-peel, and an old window-sash.

Can you believe it? Tom's plan is actually working! He's tricked all his friends into thinking that whitewashing a fence is the coolest, neatest thing to do ever! And not only are they doing his work, they're trading him their worldly wealth to do it.

He had a nice, good, idle time all the while—plenty of company—and the fence had three coats of whitewash on it! If he hadn't run out of whitewash, he would have bankrupted every boy in the village.

Tom said to himself that it was not such a hollow world, after all. He had discovered a great law of human action, without knowing it—namely, that in order to make a man or a boy want a thing, it is only necessary to make the thing difficult to reach. If he had been a great and wise philosopher, like the writer of this book, he would now have understood that Work consists of whatever a body is *forced* to do, and that Play consists of whatever a body is not forced to do.

The boy thought a while over the substantial change which had taken place in his worldly circumstances, and then went toward headquarters to report.

3
Triumph and Reward

So the fence is completely whitewashed, Tom didn't have to do one bit of work, and now he's gone to tell Aunt Polly that his punishment is completed. I'll bet he can't wait to see Aunt Polly's reaction.

Tom presented himself before Aunt Polly, who was sitting by an open window in a pleasant apartment, which was bed-room, breakfast-room, dining-room, and library, combined. The balmy summer air, the restful quiet, the odor of the flowers, and the drowsing murmur of the bees, had had their effect, and she was nodding over her knitting—for she had no company but the cat, and it was asleep in her lap. Her spectacles were propped up on her gray head for safety. She had thought that of course Tom had deserted long ago, and she wondered at seeing him place himself in her power again in this fearless way.

He said:

"Mayn't I go and play now, aunt?"

"What, a'ready? How much have you done?"

Aunt Polly has only a CAT for company? The poor woman. Where's the dog?

"It's all done, aunt."

"Tom, don't lie to me—I can't bear it."

"I ain't, aunt; it *is* all done."

Aunt Polly placed small trust in such evidence. She went out to see for herself; and she would have been content to find twenty per cent of Tom's statement true. When she found the entire fence whitewashed, and not only whitewashed but elaborately coated and recoated, and even a streak added to the ground, her astonishment was almost unspeakable.

She said:

"Well, I never! There's no getting round it, you *can* work when you're a mind to, Tom."

And then she diluted the compliment by adding:

"But it's powerful seldom you're a mind to, I'm bound to say. Well, go 'long and play; but mind you get back sometime in a week, or I'll tan you."

As he was passing by the house where Jeff Thatcher lived, he saw a new girl in the garden—a lovely little blue-eyed creature with yellow hair plaited into two long tails, white summer frock and embroidered pantalettes. The fresh-crowned hero fell without firing a shot. A certain Amy Lawrence vanished out of his heart and left not even a memory of herself behind. He had thought he loved her to distraction, he had regarded his passion as adoration. He had been months winning her; she had confessed hardly a week ago; he had been the happiest and the proudest boy in the world only seven short days, and here in one instant of time she had gone out of his heart like a casual stranger whose visit is done.

He worshiped this new angel with furtive eye, till he saw that she had discovered him; then he pretended he did not know she was present, and began to "show off" in all sorts of boyish ways, in order to win her admiration. He kept up this foolishness for some time; but by and by, while he was in the midst of some dangerous gymnastic performances, he glanced aside and saw that the little girl was making her way toward the house. Tom came up to the fence and leaned on it, grieving, and hoping she would wait yet a while longer. She halted a moment on the steps and then moved toward the door. Tom heaved a great sigh as she put her foot on the threshold. But his face lit up, right away, for she tossed a pansy over the fence a moment before she disappeared.

The boy ran around and stopped within a foot or two of the flower, and then shaded his eyes with his hand and began to look down street as if he had discovered something of interest going on in that direction. Presently he picked up a straw and began trying to balance it on his nose, with his head tilted far back; and as he moved from side to side, in his efforts, he edged nearer and nearer toward the pansy; finally, his bare foot rested upon it, his toes closed upon it, and he hopped away with the treasure and disappeared around the corner. But only for a minute—only while he could button the flower inside his jacket.

He returned, now, and hung about the fence till nightfall, "showing off," as before; but the girl never exhibited herself again, though Tom comforted himself a little with the hope that she had been near some window, meantime, and been aware of his attentions. Finally he strode home reluctantly, with his poor head full of visions.

Now this is an interesting day. Tom spends his morning getting out of work and gaining worldly wealth, only to lose his heart in the afternoon to the girl with yellow braids. How romantic! Ah, young love! Oh . . . sorry. Got carried away there.

4
Cautious Approaches

As our story continues, Monday morning has finally arrived, and Tom must go to school. Naturally, he doesn't want to. To Tom, being in school is the same thing as being put in chains and thrown into jail! We join him as he makes his weary way to the schoolhouse.

Monday morning found Tom Sawyer miserable. Monday morning always found him so—because it began another week's slow suffering in school.

Shortly Tom came upon the outcast of the village, Huckleberry Finn, son of the town drunkard. Huckleberry was cordially hated and dreaded by all the mothers of the town, because he was idle, and lawless, and vulgar and bad—and because all their children admired him so, and delighted in his forbidden society, and wished they dared to be like him. Tom was like the rest of the respectable boys, in that he envied Huckleberry his gaudy outcast condition, and was under strict orders not to play with him. So he played with him every time he got a chance. Huckleberry was always dressed in the cast-off clothes of full-grown men, and they were in perennial bloom and fluttering with rags. His hat was a vast ruin; his coat, when he wore one, hung nearly to his heels and had the rearward buttons far down the back; but one suspender supported his trousers; the seat of the trousers bagged low and contained nothing; the fringed legs dragged in the dirt when not rolled up.

Huckleberry came and went, at his own free will. He slept on door-steps in fine weather and in empty hogsheads in wet; he did not have to go to school or to church, or call any being master or obey anybody; he could go fishing or swimming when and where he chose, and stay as long as it suited him; nobody forbade him to fight; he could sit up as late as he pleased; he was always the first boy that went barefoot in the spring and the last to resume leather in the fall, he never had to wash, nor put on clean clothes; he could swear wonderfully. In a word, everything that goes to make life precious, that boy had. So thought every harassed, hampered, respectable boy in St. Petersburg.

What an adventurous life Huck Finn must lead! No work, no school, goes barefoot all the time, and even sleeps in hogsheads! (Those are big barrels.) It seems to me that Huck is popular with all the boys for the same reasons he is unpopular with all the grown-ups!

Tom hailed the romantic outcast:

"Hello, Huckleberry!"

"Hello yourself, and see how you like it."

"What's that you got?"

"Dead cat."

"Lemme see him, Huck. My, he's a pretty stiff. Where'd you get him?"

"Bought him off'n a boy."

"Say—what is dead cats good for, Huck?"

"Good for? Cure warts with."

"No! Is that so? How do you cure 'em with dead cats?"

"Why, you take your cat, and go and get in the graveyard 'long about midnight, when somebody that was wicked has been buried; and when it's midnight a devil will come, or maybe two or three, but you can't see 'em, you can only hear something like the wind, or maybe hear 'em talk; and when they're taking that feller away, you heave your cat after 'em, and say, 'Devil follow corpse, cat follow devil, warts follow cat, *I'm* done with ye!' That'll fetch *any* wart."

By the way, a corpse is a dead body. Spooky, huh?

"Sounds right. Say, Hucky, when you going to try the cat?"

"Tonight. I reckon they'll come after old Hoss Williams tonight."

"But they buried him Saturday. Didn't they get him Saturday night?"

"Why how you talk! How could their charms work till midnight?—and *then* its Sunday. Devils don't slosh around much of a Sunday, I don't reckon."

"I never thought of that. That's so. Lemme go with you?"

"Of course—if you ain't afeard."

"Afeard! 'Taint likely. Will you meow?"

"Yes—and you meow back, if you get a chance. Last time, you kep' me a meowing around till old Hays went to throwing rocks at me and says 'Dern that cat!' and so I hove a brick through his window—but don't you tell."

"I won't. I couldn't meow that night, becuz aunty was watching me, but I'll meow this time."

• • • • • •

When Tom reached the little isolated frame Schoolhouse, he strode in briskly, with the manner of one who had come with all honest speed. He hung his hat on a peg and flung himself into his seat. The master throned on high in his great splint-bottom arm chair, was dozing, lulled by the drowsy hum of study. **In Mark Twain's day, teachers were called "masters" or "schoolmasters."** The interruption roused him.

"Thomas Sawyer!"

Tom knew that when his name was pronounced in full, it meant trouble.

"Sir!"

"Come up here. Now sir, why are you late again, as usual?"

Tom was about to take refuge in a lie, when he saw two long tails of yellow hair hanging down a back that he recognized by electric sympathy of love; and by that form was *the only vacant place* on the girl's side of the school-house. He instantly said:

"I STOPPED TO TALK WITH HUCKLEBERRY FINN!"

Tom sees that there is an empty place next to the girl who has stolen his heart. Tom knows if he gets into trouble his punishment will be to sit with the girls, which means he will get to sit next to her! So he says what he knows will get him into BIG trouble.

The master's pulse stood still, and he stared helplessly. The buzz of study ceased. The pupils wondered if this fool-hardy boy had lost his mind. The master said:

"You—you did what?"

"Stopped to talk with Huckleberry Finn."

There was no mistaking the words.

"Thomas Sawyer, this is the most astounding confession I have ever listened to. Sir, go and sit with the *girls*! And let this be a warning to you."

The giggle that rippled around the room appeared to embarrass the boy, but in reality that result was caused rather more by his worshipful awe of his unknown idol and the dread-pleasure that lay in his high good fortune. He sat down upon the end of the pine bench and the girl hitched herself away from him with a toss of her head. Nudges and winks and whispers traversed the room, but Tom sat still, with his arms upon the long, low desk before him, and seemed to study his book.

By and by attention ceased from him, and the accustomed school murmur rose upon the dull air once more. Presently the boy began to steal furtive glances at the girl. She observed it, "made a mouth" at him and gave him the back of her head for the space of a minute. When she cautiously faced around again, a peach lay before her. She thrust it away. Tom gently put it back. She thrust it away, again, but with less hostility. Tom patiently returned it to its place. Then she let it remain. Tom scrawled on his slate, "Please take it—I got more." **Wow! He's offering her the greatest gift—a snack!** The girl glanced at the words, but made no sign. Now the boy began to draw something on the slate, hiding his work with his left hand. For a time the girl refused to notice; but her human curiosity presently began to manifest itself by hardly perceptible signs. The boy worked on, apparently unconscious. The girl made a sort of non-commital attempt to see, but the boy did not betray that he was aware of it. At last she gave in and hesitatingly whispered:

"Let me see it."

Tom partly uncovered a clumsy drawing of a house with two gable ends to it and a cork-screw of smoke issuing from the chimney. Then the girl's interest began to fasten itself upon the work and she forgot everything else. When it was finished, she gazed a moment, then whispered:

"It's nice—make a man."

The artist erected a man in the front yard. He could have stepped over the house; but the girl was not hypercritical; she was satisfied with the monster, and whispered:

"It's a beautiful man—now make me coming along."

Tom drew an hour-glass with a full moon and straw limbs to it and armed the spreading fingers with a huge fan. The girl said:

"It's ever so nice—I wish I could draw."

"It's easy," whispered Tom, "I'll learn you."

"O, will you? When?"

"At noon. Do you go home to dinner?"

"I'll stay if you will."

"Good—that's a whack. What's your name?"

"Becky Thatcher. What's yours? Oh, I know. It's Thomas Sawyer."

"That's the name they lick me by. I'm Tom when I'm good. You call me Tom, will you?"

"Yes."

Now Tom began to scrawl something on the slate, hiding the words from the girl. But she was not backward this time. She begged to see. Tom said:

"Oh, it ain't anything."

"Yes it is."

"No it ain't. You don't want to see."

"Yes I do, indeed I do. Please let me."

"You'll tell."

"No I won't—deed and deed and double deed I won't."

"You won't tell anybody at all? Ever, as long as you live?"

"No I won't ever tell anybody. Now let me."

"Oh, *you* don't want to see!"

"Now that you treat me so, I *will* see."

And she put her small hand upon his and a little scuffle ensued, Tom pretending to resist in earnest, but letting his hand slip by degrees until these words were revealed:

"*I love you.*"

"O, you bad thing!"

And she hit his hand a smart rap, but reddened and looked pleased, nevertheless.

Just at this point the boy felt a slow, fateful grip closing on his ear, and a steady lifting impulse. In that vise he was borne across the house and deposited in his own seat, under a peppering fire of giggles from the whole school. Then the master stood over him during a few awful moments, and finally moved away to his throne without saying a word. But although Tom's ear tingled, his heart was joyful.

As the school quieted down Tom made an honest effort to study, but the turmoil within him was too great. In turn he took his place in the reading class and made a botch of it; then in the geography class, and turned lakes into mountains, mountains into rivers, and rivers into continents, till chaos was come again; then in the spelling class, and got "turned down," by a succession of mere baby words.

Poor Tom is so crazy about Becky, he can't remember how to spell! But he's got her attention, and that's the important thing. Now . . . will he be able to keep it?

5
A Mistake Made

Back in the days before school lunch, kids always went home to eat. But on this particular day, Tom Sawyer has a plan. He and Becky, the new love of his life, will pretend they're going home for lunch, then sneak back to the schoolyard to spend time together. Romantic, isn't it?

When school broke up at noon, Tom flew to Becky Thatcher and whispered in her ear:

"Put on your bonnet, and let on you're going home; and when you get to the corner, give the rest of 'em the slip, and turn down through the lane and come back."

So the one went off with one group of scholars, and the other with another. In a little while the two met at the bottom of the lane, and when they reached the school they had it all to themselves. Then they sat together, with a slate before them, and Tom gave Becky the pencil, and held her hand in his, guiding it, and so created another surprising house. When the interest in art began to wane, the two fell to talking. Tom was swimming in bliss. He said:

"Do you love rats?"

"No! I hate them!"

"Well, I do, too—*live* ones. But I mean dead ones, to swing around your head with a string."

"No, I don't care for rats much, anyway. What *I* like is chewing-gum."

"O, I should say so! I wish I had some now."

"Do you? I've got some. I'll let you chew it a while, but you must give it back to me."

That was agreeable, so they chewed it turn about, and dangled their legs against the bench in excess of contentment.

"Was you ever at a circus?" said Tom.

"Yes, and my pa's going to take me again some time, if I'm good."

"I been to the circus three or four times—lots of times. There's things going on at the circus all the time. I'm going to be a clown in a circus when I grow up."

"O, are you! That will be nice. They're so lovely, all spotted up."

"Yes, that's so. And they get lots of money—most a dollar a day, Ben Rogers says. Say, Becky, was you ever engaged?"

"What's that?"

"Why, engaged to be married."

"No."

"Would you like to?"

"I reckon so. I don't know. What is it like?"

"Like? Why it ain't like anything. You only just tell a boy you won't ever have anybody but him, ever, ever, *ever*, and then you kiss and that's all. Anybody can do it."

"Kiss? What do you kiss for?"

"Why that, you know, is to—well, they always do that."

"Everybody?"

"Why yes, everybody that's in love with each other. Do you remember what I wrote on the slate?"

"Ye—yes."

"What was it?"

"I shan't tell you."

"Shall I tell *you*?"

"Ye—yes—but some other time."

"No, now."

"No, not now—tomorrow."

"O, no, *now*. Please Becky—I'll whisper it, I'll whisper it ever so easy."

Becky hesitating, Tom took silence for consent, and passed his arm around her waist and whispered the tale ever so softly, with his mouth close to her ear. And then he added:

"Now you whisper it to me—just the same."

She resisted, for a while, and then said:

"You turn your face away so you can't see, and then I will. But you mustn't ever tell anybody—*will* you, Tom? Now you won't, *will* you?"

"No, indeed; indeed, I won't. Now Becky."

He turned his face away. She bent timidly around till her breath stirred his curls and whispered:

"I—love—you."

Then she sprang away and ran around and around the desks and benches, with Tom after her, and took refuge in a corner at last, with her little white apron to her face. Tom clasped her about the neck and pleaded:

"Now Becky, it's all done—all over but the kiss. Don't you be afraid of that—it ain't anything at all. Please, Becky."

And he tugged at her apron and the hands.

By and by she gave up, and let her hands drop; her

face, all glowing with the struggle, came up and submitted. Tom kissed the red lips, and said:

"Now it's all done, Becky. And always after this, you know, you ain't ever to love anybody but me, and you ain't ever to marry anybody but me, never, never, and forever. Will you?"

"No, I'll never love anybody but you, Tom, and I'll never marry anybody but you—and you ain't to ever marry anybody but me, either."

"Certainly. Of course. That's *part* of it. And always coming to school or when we're going home, you're to walk with me, when there ain't anybody looking—and you choose me and I choose you at parties, because that's the way you do when you're engaged."

"It's so nice. I never heard of it before."

"Oh its ever so fun! Why me and Amy Lawrence— "

The big eyes told Tom his blunder and he stopped, confused.

"O, Tom! Then I ain't the first you've ever been engaged to!"

The child began to cry. Tom said:

"O, don't cry, Becky; I don't care for her any more."

"Yes you do, Tom—you know you do."

Tom tried to put his arm about her neck, but she pushed him away and turned her face to the wall, and went on crying. Tom tried again, with soothing words in his mouth, and was repulsed again. Then his pride was up, and he strode away and went outside. He stood about, restless and uneasy, for a while, glancing at the door, every now and then, hoping she would repent and come to find him. But she did not. Then he began to feel badly and fear that he was in the wrong. It was a hard struggle with him to make new advances, now, but he nerved himself to it and entered. She was still standing back there in the corner, sobbing, with her face to the wall. Tom's heart smote him. He went to her and stood a moment, not knowing exactly how to proceed. Then he said, hesitatingly:

"Becky, I—I don't care for anybody but you."

No reply—but sobs.

"Becky," pleadingly. "Becky, won't you say something?"

More sobs.

Tom got out his chiefest jewel, a brass knob, and passed it around her so that she could see it, and said:

"Please, Becky, won't you take it?"

She struck it to the floor. Then Tom marched out of the house and over the hills and far away, to return to school no more that day. Presently Becky began to suspect. She ran to the door; he was not in sight; she flew around to the play-yard; he was not there. Then she called:

"Tom! Come back, Tom!"

She listened intently, but there was no answer. She had no companions but silence and loneliness. So she sat down to cry again and blame herself; and by this time the scholars began to gather again, and she had to hide her griefs and still her broken heart and take up the cross of a long, dreary, aching afternoon, with none among the strangers about her to exchange sorrows with.

That's the thing about new love. Sooner or later, you're going to have that "first argument." Becky's pretty upset, and Tom is, too, but he tries not to show it. He may not have time to think too much about it, though, since he's got an appointment with Huck Finn . . . at midnight . . . in the graveyard.

6
Grave Subjects Introduced

Tom was so upset by Becky that he played hookey from school and spent the afternoon playing Robin Hood with his friend Joe Harper. Later that evening he is lying in bed, waiting for Huck to give him the signal to start on their adventure in the graveyard.

At half-past nine, that night, Tom and Sid were sent to bed, as usual. They said their prayers, and Sid was soon asleep. Tom lay awake, and waited in restless impatience. When it seemed to him that it must be nearly daylight, he heard the clock strike ten! This was despair. He would have tossed and fidgeted, as his nerves demanded, but he was afraid he might wake Sid. So he lay still, and stared up into the dark. Everything was dismally still. By and by, out of the stillness, little, scarcely perceptibly noises began to emphasize themselves. The ticking of the clock began to bring itself into notice. Old beams began to crack mysteriously. The stairs creaked faintly. Evidently spirits were abroad. A measured, muffled snore issued from Aunt Polly's chamber. Then the howl of a far-off dog rose on the night air, and was answered by a fainter howl from a remoter distance. Tom was in agony. **I'll bet he is! How can he sit with all that activity going on? Of course, in the daytime, you might not even notice sounds like a ticking clock or a howling dog.**

But at night, lying alone in the dark, waiting anxiously for an adventure to begin—well, that's when little noises can start to sound big. At last he was satisfied that time had ceased and eternity begun; he began to doze, in spite of himself; the clock chimed eleven, but he did not hear it. And then there came mingling with his half-formed dreams a most melancholy howl—the howl of a cat. The raising of a neighboring window disturbed him. A cry of "Scat! you devil!" and the crash of an empty bottle against the back of his aunt's woodshed brought him wide awake, and a single minute later he was dressed and out of the window, and creeping along the roof of the "ell" on all fours. He "meow'd" with caution once or twice, as he went; then jumped to the roof of the woodshed, and thence to the ground. Huckleberry Finn was there, with his dead cat. The boys moved off and disappeared in the gloom. At the end of half an hour they were wading through the tall grass of the graveyard.

It was a graveyard of the old-fashioned western kind. It was on a hill, about a mile and a half from the village. It had a crazy board fence around it, which leaned inward in places, and outward the rest of the time, but stood upright nowhere. Grass and weeds grew rank over the whole cemetery. All the old graves were sunken in, there was not a tombstone on the place; round-topped, worm-eaten boards staggered over the graves, leaning for support and finding none. "Sacred to the memory of" So-and-so had been painted on them once, but it could no longer have been read, on the most of them, now, even if there had been light.

A faint wind moaned through the trees, and Tom feared it might be the spirits of the dead, complaining at being disturbed. The boys talked little, and only under their breath, for the time and the place oppressed their spirits. They found the sharp new heap they were seeking, and settled themselves within the protection of three great elms that grew in a bunch within a few feet of the grave.

Then they waited in silence for what seemed a long time. The hooting of a distant owl was all the sound that troubled the dead stillness. Tom's reflections grew oppressive. He must force some talk. So he said in a whisper:

"Hucky, do you believe the dead people like it for us to be here?"

Huckleberry whispered:

"I wisht I knowed. It's awful solemn like, *ain't* it?"

"I bet it is."

There was a considerable pause, while the boys examined this matter inwardly. Then Tom whispered:

"Say, Hucky—do you reckon Hoss Williams hears us talking?"

"O' course he does. Least his sperrit does."

Tom, after a pause:

"I wish I'd said *Mister* Williams. But I never meant any harm. Everybody calls him Hoss."

"A body can't be too partic'lar how they talk 'bout these-yer dead people, Tom."

This was a damper, and conversation died again. Presently Tom seized his comrade's arm and said:

"Sh!"

A comrade is a friend. You know, a buddy, a pal, a companion, a . . . well, you get the idea.

"What is it, Tom?" And the two clung together with beating hearts.

"Sh! There 'tis again! Didn't you hear it?"

"I—"

"There! Now you hear it!"

"Lord, Tom they're coming! They're coming, sure. What'll we do?"

"I dono. Think they'll see us?"

"O, Tom, they can see in the dark, same as cats. I wisht I hadn't come."

"O, don't be afeard. *I* don't believe they'll bother us. We ain't doing any harm. If we keep perfectly still, maybe they won't notice us at all."

"I'll try to, Tom, but Lord I'm all of a shiver."

"Listen!"

The boys bent their heads together and scarcely breathed. A muffled sound of voices floated up from the far end of the graveyard.

"Look! See there!" whispered Tom. "What is it?"

"It's devil-fire. O, Tom, this is awful."

Some vague figures approached through the gloom, swinging an old-fashioned tin lantern that freckled the ground with little spangles of light. Presently Huckleberry whispered with a shudder:

"It's the devils sure enough. Three of 'em! Lordy, Tom, we're goners! Can you pray?"

"I'll try, but don't you be afeard. They ain't going to hurt us. Now I lay me down to sleep, I—"

"Sh!"

"What is it, Huck?"

"They're *humans*! One of 'em is, anyway. One of 'em's old Muff Potter's voice."

"No—tain't so, is it?"

"I bet I know it. Don't you stir nor budge. *He* ain't sharp enough to notice us. Drunk, same as usual, likely— blamed old rip!"

"All right, I'll keep still. Now they're stuck. Can't find it. Here they come again. Now they're hot. Cold again. Hot again. Red hot! They're p'inted right, this time. Say Huck, I know another o' them voices; it's Injun Joe."

"That's so—that murderin' half-breed! I'd druther they was devils a dern sight. What kin they be up to?"

The whispers died wholly out, now, for the three men had reached the grave and stood within a few feet of the boys' hiding-place.

"Here it is," said the third voice; and the owner of it held the lantern up and revealed the face of young Dr. Robinson.

Potter and Injun Joe were carrying a handbarrow with a rope and a couple of shovels on it. They cast down their load and began to open the grave. The doctor put the lantern at the head of the grave and came and sat down with his back against one of the elm trees. He was so close the boys could have touched him.

"Hurry, men!" he said, in a low voice; "the moon might come out at any moment."

These men are grave robbers! Grave robbers would dig up graves to steal valuables or to get bodies for medical experiments. Very creepy.

They growled a response and went on digging. For some time there was no noise but the grating sound of the shovels discharging their freight of mould

43

and gravel. Finally a shovel struck upon the coffin with a dull woody accent, and within another minute or two the men had lifted it out on the ground. They pried off the lid with their shovels, got out the body and dumped it rudely on the ground. The moon drifted from behind the clouds and exposed the pale face. The barrow was got ready and the corpse placed on it, covered with a blanket, and bound to its place with the rope. Potter took out a large spring-knife and cut off the dangling end of the rope and then said:

"Now the cussed thing's ready, Sawbones, and you'll just out with another five, or here she stays."

Sawbones is a slang word for doctor.

"That's the talk!" said Injun Joe.

"Look here, what does this mean?" said the doctor. "You required your pay in advance, and I've paid you."

"Yes, and you done more than that," said Injun Joe, approaching the doctor, who was now standing. "Five years ago you drove me away from your father's kitchen one night, when I come to ask for something to eat, and you said I warn't there for any good; and when I swore I'd get even with you if it took a hundred years, your father had me jailed for a vagrant. Did you think I'd forget? The Injun blood ain't in me for nothing. And now I've *got* you, and you got to *settle*, you know!"

He was threatening the doctor, with his fist in his face, by this time. The doctor struck out suddenly and stretched the ruffian on the ground. Potter dropped his knife and exclaimed:

"Here, now, don't you hit my pard!" and the next moment he had grappled with the doctor and the two were struggling with might and main, trampling the grass and tearing the ground with their heels. **Potter is defending his**

"pard," or his partner. You know, his comrade, his buddy, his pal, his . . . well, you get the idea. Injun Joe sprang to his feet, his eyes flaming with passion, snatched up Potter's knife, and went creeping, catlike and stooping, round and round about the combatants, seeking an opportunity. All at once the doctor flung himself free, seized the heavy head board of Williams' grave and knocked Potter to the earth with it— and in the same instant Injun Joe saw his chance and drove the knife to the hilt in the young doctor's breast. He reeled and fell partly upon Potter, flooding him with his blood, and in the same moment the clouds blotted out the

dreadful spectacle and the two frightened boys went speeding away in the dark.

Presently, when the moon emerged again, Injun Joe was standing over the two forms, contemplating them. The doctor murmured, gave a long gasp or two and was still. The half-breed muttered:

"*That* score is settled."

Then he robbed the body. After which he put the fatal knife in Potter's open right hand, and sat down on the dismantled coffin. Three—four—five minutes passed, and then Potter began to stir and moan. His hand closed upon the knife; he raised it, glanced at it, and let it fall, with a shudder. Then he sat up, pushing the body from him, and gazed at it, and then around him, confusedly. His eyes met Joe's.

"Lord, how is this, Joe?" he said.

"It's a dirty business," said Joe, without moving. "What did you do it for?"

"I! I never done it!"

"Look here! That kind of talk won't wash."

Potter trembled and grew white.

"I thought I'd got sober. I'd no business to drink tonight. I'm all in a muddle; can't recollect anything of it hardly. Tell me, Joe—*honest*, now, old feller—did I do it? Joe, I never meant to—'pon my soul and honor, I never meant to, Joe. Tell me how it was, Joe. O, it's awful—and him so young and promising."

"Why you two was scuffling, and he fetched you one with the head-board and you fell flat; and then up you come, all reeling and staggering, like, and snatched the knife and jammed it into him, just as he fetched you another awful clip—and here you've laid."

"O, I didn't know what I was doing. I wish I may die this minute if I did. It was all on account of the whiskey; and the excitement, I reckon. I never used a weepon in my life before, Joe. I've fought, but never with weepons. They'll all say that. Joe, don't tell! Say you won't tell, Joe—that's a good feller. I always liked you, Joe, and stood up for you, too. Don't you remember? You *won't* tell, *will* you Joe?" And the poor creature dropped on his knees before the stolid murderer, and clasped his appealing hands.

"No, you've always been fair and square with me, Muff Potter, and I won't go back on you. There, now, that's as fair as a man can say."

"O, Joe, you're an angel. I'll bless you for this the longest day I live." And Potter began to cry.

"Come, now, that's enough of that. This ain't any time for blubbering. You be off yonder way and I'll go this. Move, now, and don't leave any tracks behind you."

Potter started on a trot that quickly increased to a run. The half-breed stood looking after him.

He muttered:

"He won't think of the knife till he's gone so far he'll be afraid to come back after it to such a place by himself—chicken heart!"

Two or three minutes later the murdered man, the blanketed corpse, the lidless coffin and the open grave were under no inspection but the moon's. The stillness was complete again, too.

7
The Solemn Oath

Murder in the graveyard! Tom and Huck just wanted to cure some warts, but now they're in trouble up to their eyeballs! The boys witnessed Injun Joe murder Doc Robinson. Then they saw Joe set up his "pard," Muff Potter, to take the blame. There was only one thing left for our young heroes to do—RUN!

The two boys flew on and on, toward the village, speechless with horror. They glanced backward over their shoulders from time to time, as if they feared they might be followed. Every stump that started up in their path seemed a man and an enemy, and made them catch their breath; and as they sped by some outlying cottages that lay near the village, the barking of the aroused watch-dogs seemed to give wings to their feet.

"If we can only get to the old tannery, before we break down!" whispered Tom, in short catches between breaths, "I can't stand it much longer."

Huckleberry's hard pantings were his only reply, and the boys fixed their eyes on the goal of their hopes and bent to their work to win it. They gained steadily on it, and at last, breast to breast they burst through the open door and fell grateful and exhausted in the sheltering shadows beyond. By and by their pulses slowed down, and Tom whispered:

"Huckleberry, what do you reckon 'll come of this?"

"If Dr. Robinson dies, I reckon hanging 'll come of it."

"Do you though?"

"Why, I *know* it, Tom."

Tom thought a while, then he said: "Who'll tell? We?"

"What are you talking about? S'pose something happened and Injun Joe *didn't* hang! Why he'd kill us some time or other, just as dead sure as we're a laying here."

"That's just what I was thinking to myself, Huck."

"If anybody tells, let Muff Potter do it, if he's fool enough. He's generally drunk enough."

Tom said nothing—went on thinking. Presently whispered:

"Huck, Muff Potter don't *know* it. How can he tell?"

"What's the reason he don't know it?"

"Because he'd just got that whack when Injun Joe done it. D'you reckon he could see anything? D'you reckon he knowd anything?"

"By hokey, that's so Tom!"

"And besides, look-a-here—maybe that whack done *him*!"

"No, 'taint likely Tom. He had liquor in him; I could see that; and besides, he always has. Well when pap's full, you might take and belt him over the head with a church and you couldn't phase him. He says so, his own self. So it's the same with Muff Potter, of course. But if a man was dead sober, I reckon maybe that whack might fetch him; I dono."

After another reflective silence, Tom said:

"Hucky, you sure you can keep mum?"

"Tom, we *got* to keep mum. *You* know that. That Injun devil wouldn't make any more of drownding us than a couple of cats, if we was to squeak 'bout this and they didn't hang him. Now look-a-here, Tom, less take and swear to one another—that's what we got to do—swear to keep mum."

"I'm agreed. It's the best thing. Would you just hold hands and swear that we—"

"O, no, that wouldn't do for this. That's good enough for little rubbishy common things—specially with gals, cuz *they* go back on you anyway, and blab if they get in a huff—but there orter be writing 'bout a big thing like this. And blood."

Tom's whole being applauded this idea. It was deep, and dark, and awful; the hour, the circumstances, the surroundings, were in keeping with it. He picked up a clean pine shingle that lay in the moonlight, took a little fragment of "red keel" out of his pocket, got the moon on his work, and painfully scrawled these lines, emphasizing each slow down-stroke by clamping his tongue between his teeth, and letting up the pressure on the up-strokes: **Red keel is an earthy mixture used for writing.**

Huck Finn and Tom Sawyer swears they will keep mum about this and they wish they may drop down dead in their tracks if they ever tell and rot.

Huckleberry was filled with admiration of Tom's skill in writing.

Each boy pricked the ball of his thumb and squeezed out a drop of blood. In time, after many squeezes, Tom managed to sign his initials, using the ball of his little finger for a pen. Then he showed Huckleberry how to make an H and an F, and the oath was complete. They buried the shingle close to the wall.

"Tom," whispered Huckleberry, "does this keep us from *ever* telling—*always*?"

"Of course it does. It don't make any difference *what* happens, we got to keep mum. We'd drop down dead—don't *you* know that?"

"Yes, I reckon that's so."

They continued to whisper for some little time.

That's a big secret for two boys to try to keep. Tom and Huck left the tannery, and Tom quietly snuck home.

When Tom crept in at his bedroom window, the night was almost spent. He undressed with excessive caution, and fell asleep congratulating himself that nobody knew of his escapade. He was not aware that the gently-snoring Sid was awake, and had been so for an hour.

When Tom awoke, Sid was dressed and gone. There was a late look in the light, a late sense in the atmosphere. He was startled. Why had he not been called? The thought filled him with bodings. Within five minutes he was dressed and down stairs, feeling sore and drowsy. The family were still at table, but they had finished breakfast. There was no voice of disapproval; but there were averted eyes; there was a silence and an air of solemnity that struck a chill to the culprit's heart. He sat down and tried to seem happy, but it was up-hill work; it roused no smile, no response, and he lapsed into silence and let his heart sink down to the depths.

After breakfast his aunt took him aside, and Tom almost brightened in the hope that he was going to be flogged; but it was not so. His aunt wept over him and asked him how he could go and break her old heart so; and finally told him to go on, and ruin himself and bring her gray hairs with sorrow to the grave, for it was no use for her to try any more. This was worse than a thousand whippings, and Tom's heart was sorer now than his body. He cried, he pleaded for forgiveness, promised reform over and over again, and then received his dismissal.

Tattletale Sid told Aunt Polly that Tom was out prowling around during the night. Aunt Polly got so mad at Tom, she didn't know WHAT to do. Tom feels really bad about that.

He left the presence too miserable to even feel revengeful toward Sid. He moped to school gloomy and sad. Then he betook himself to his seat, rested his elbows on his desk and his jaws in his hands and stared at the wall with the stony stare of suffering that has reached the limit and can no further go. His elbow was pressing against some hard substance. After a long time he slowly and sadly changed his position, and took up this object with a sigh. It was in a paper. He unrolled it. A long, lingering, colossal sigh followed, and his heart broke. It was his brass knob!

This final feather broke the camel's back.

It's just been one of those days for Tom. He witnessed a murder—which he has to keep a secret—he made Aunt Polly cry, and now this! His prize brass knob has been returned to him by the person he wanted most to have it—Becky. Having Becky mad at him is "the final feather that broke the camel's back."

8

Tom's Conscience at Work

Meanwhile, back in town, the news of Doc Robinson's murder is spreading faster than a dog chasing an alley cat!

Close upon the hour of noon the whole village was suddenly electrified with the ghastly news. The tale flew from man to man, from group to group, from house to house, with little less than telegraphic speed. Of course the schoolmaster gave holiday for that afternoon; the town would have thought strangely of him if he had not.

A gory knife had been found close to the murdered man, and it had been recognized by somebody as belonging to Muff Potter—so the story ran. And it was said that a belated citizen had come upon Potter washing himself in the brook about one or two o'clock in the morning, and that Potter had at once sneaked off—suspicious circumstances, especially the washing, which was not a habit with Potter. It was also said that the town had been ransacked for this "murderer" (the public are not slow in the matter of sifting evidence and arriving at a verdict), but that he could not be found. Horsemen had departed down all the roads in every direction, and the sheriff "was confident" that he would be captured before night.

All the town was drifting toward the graveyard. Tom's heartbreak vanished and he joined the procession, not because he would not a thousand times rather go anywhere else, but because an awful, unaccountable fascination drew him on. Arrived at the dreadful place, he wormed his small body through the crowd and saw the dismal spectacle. It seemed to him an age since he was there before. Somebody pinched his arm. He turned, and his eyes met Huckleberry's. Then both looked elsewhere at once, and wondered if anybody had noticed any thing in their mutual glance. But everybody was talking, and intent upon the grisly spectacle before them.

"Poor fellow!" "Poor young fellow!" "This ought to be a lesson to grave robbers!" "Muff Potter'll hang for this if they catch him!" This was the drift of remarks.

Now Tom shivered from head to heel; for his eye fell upon the stolid face of Injun Joe. At this moment the crowd began to sway and struggle, and voices shouted, "It's him! it's him! he's coming himself!"

"Who? Who?" from twenty voices.

"Muff Potter!"

"Hallo, he's stopped! Look out, he's turning! Don't let him get away!"

People in the branches of the trees over Tom's head, said he wasn't trying to get away—he only looked doubtful and perplexed.

The crowd fell apart, now, and the sheriff came through, leading Potter by the arm. The poor fellow's face was haggard, and his eyes showed the fear that was upon him. When he stood before the murdered man, he shook as with a palsy, and he put his face in his hands, and burst into tears.

"I didn't do it, friends," he sobbed; " 'pon my word and honor, I never done it."

"Who's accused you?" shouted a voice.

This shot seemed to carry home. Potter lifted his face and looked around him with a pathetic hopelessness in his eyes. He saw Injun Joe, and exclaimed:

"O, Injun Joe, you promised me you'd never—"

"Is that your knife?" and it was thrust before him by the sheriff.

Potter would have fallen if they had not caught him and eased him to the ground. Then he said:

"Something told me 't if I didn't come back and get—"

He shuddered; then waved his nerveless hand with a vanquished gesture and said:

"Tell 'em, Joe, tell 'em—it ain't any use any more."

Then Huckleberry and Tom stood dumb and staring, and heard the stony hearted liar reel off his serene statement, they expecting every moment that the clear sky would deliver God's lightnings upon his head, and wondering to see how long the stroke was delayed. And when he had finished and still stood alive and whole, their wavering impulse to break their oath and save the poor betrayed prisoner's life faded and vanished away, for plainly this villain had sold himself to Satan and it would be fatal to meddle with the property of such a power as that.

"Why didn't you leave? What did you want to come here for?" somebody said.

"I couldn't help it—I couldn't help it," Potter moaned. "I wanted to run away, but I couldn't seem to come anywhere but here."

And he fell to sobbing again.

Injun Joe repeated his statement, just as calmly, a few minutes afterward on the inquest, under oath; and the boys, seeing that the lightnings were still withheld, were confirmed in their belief that Joe had sold himself to the devil. He was now become, to them, the most balefully interesting object they had ever looked upon, and they could not take their fascinated eyes from his face.

They inwardly resolved to watch him, nights, when opportunity should offer, in the hope of getting a glimpse of his dread master.

Tom's fearful secret and gnawing conscience disturbed his sleep for as much as a week after this; and at breakfast one morning Sid said:

"Tom, you pitch around and talk in your sleep so much that you keep me awake about half the time."

Tom blanched and dropped his eyes.

"It's a bad sign," said Aunt Polly, gravely. "What you got on your mind, Tom?"

"Nothing. Nothing 't I know of." But the boy's hand shook so that he spilled his coffee.

"And you do talk such stuff," Sid said. "Last night you said 'it's blood, it's blood, that's what it is!' You said that over and over. And you said, 'Don't torment me so—I'll tell!' Tell *what*? What is it you'll tell?"

Everything was swimming before Tom. There is no telling what might have happened, now, but luckily the

Tom's conscience is bothering him, so he's having trouble sleeping.

concern passed out of Aunt Polly's face and she came to Tom's relief without knowing it. She said:

"Sho! It's that dreadful murder. I dream about it almost every night myself. Sometimes I dream it's me that done it."

Mary said she had been affected much the same way. **Mary is Tom's kind-hearted cousin.** Sid seemed satisfied. Tom got out of the presence as quick as he could, and after that he complained of toothache for a week, and tied up his jaws every night. **People had some pretty strange ideas about toothaches in those days. They thought you should tie a bandage around your mouth to keep your jaws shut, and that way, your tooth wouldn't ache. Of course, Tom doesn't really have a toothache—he's just afraid of talking in his sleep!** He never knew that Sid lay nightly watching, and frequently slipped the bandage free and then leaned on his elbow listening a good while at a time, and afterward slipped the bandage back to its place again. Tom's distress of mind wore off gradually and the toothache grew irksome and was discarded. If Sid really managed to make anything out of Tom's disjointed mutterings, he kept it to himself.

Every day or two, during this time of sorrow, Tom watched his opportunity and went to the little grated jail-window and smuggled such small comforts through to the "murderer" as he could get hold of. The jail was a trifling little brick den that stood in a marsh at the edge of the village, and no guards were afforded for it; indeed it was seldom occupied. These offerings greatly helped to ease Tom's conscience.

Poor Muff Potter. We know he's innocent, but he's the one in jail!

9
The Young Pirates

As if Tom didn't have enough troubles, along came another one: Becky became ill and stopped coming to school. This gets Tom so worried that Aunt Polly thought he was sick, and she tried all kinds of awful potions on him. Tom wasn't sick, but he was desperate to win back Becky's affection. To make matters worse, when Becky did get well enough to return to school, she simply ignored Tom and called him a "show-off." Tom was gloomy. He decided along with Joe and Huck to run off to Jackson Island to become a pirate. That night, at midnight, the boys took off to the island.

About two o'clock in the morning their raft grounded on the bar two hundred yards above the head of the island, and they waded back and forth until they had landed their freight. Each boy had brought hooks and lines, and such provisions as he could steal in the most dark and mysterious way — as become outlaws. Their raft's belongings also consisted of an old sail, and this they spread over a nook in the bushes for a tent to shelter their provisions; but they themselves would sleep in the open air in good weather, as became outlaws. **Provisions are supplies, especially the most important item—food.**

They built a fire against the side of a great log twenty or thirty steps within the somber depths of the forest, and then cooked some bacon in the frying-pan for supper, and used up half of the corn "pone" stock they had brought. It seemed glorious sport to be feasting in that wild free way in the virgin forest of an unexplored and uninhabited island, far from the haunts of men, and they said they never would return to civilization. The climbing fire lit up their faces and threw its ruddy glare upon the pillared tree trunks of their forest temple.

When the last crisp slice of bacon was gone, and the last allowance of corn pone eaten, the boys stretched themselves out on the grass, filled with contentment. They could have found a cooler place, but they would not deny themselves such a romantic feature as the roasting campfire.

"*Ain't* it fun?" said Joe.

"It's *nuts*!" said Tom. "What would the boys say if they could see us?"

"Say? Well they'd just die to be here—hey Hucky!"

"I reckon so," said Huckleberry; "anyways *I*'m suited. I don't want nothing better'n this. I don't ever get enough to eat, gen'ally—and here they can't come and pick at a feller and bullyrag him so."

"It's just the life for me," said Tom. "You don't have to get up, mornings, and you don't have to go to school, and wash, and all that blamed foolishness."

Presently Huck said:

"What does pirates have to do?"

Tom said:

"Oh, they have just a bully time—take ships and burn them, and get the money and bury it in awful places in their island, where there's ghosts and things to watch it, and kill everybody in the ships—make 'em walk a plank." **In some of the pirate stories Tom has read, prisoners have to "walk the plank." They had to walk out on a wooden board suspended over the ocean. Then the pirates forced them to jump—usually straight into shark-infested waters!**

"And they carry the women to the island," said Joe; "they don't kill the women."

"No," agreed Tom, "they don't kill the women—they're too noble. And the women's always beautiful, too."

"And don't they wear the bulliest clothes! Oh, no! All gold and silver and di'monds," said Joe, with enthusiasm.

"Who," said Huck.

"Why, the pirates."

Huck scanned his clothing forlornly.

"I reckon I ain't dressed fitten for a pirate," said he, "but I ain't got none but these."

But the other boys told him the fine clothes would come fast enough, after they should have begun their adventures. They made him understand that his poor rags would do to begin with, though it was customary for wealthy pirates to start with a proper wardrobe.

Gradually their talk died out, and drowsiness began to steal upon the eyelids of the little waifs. Huck slept the sleep of the conscience-free and the weary. Joe and Tom had more difficulty in getting to sleep. They said their prayers inwardly, and lying down, since there was nobody there with authority to make them kneel and recite aloud; in truth, they had a mind not to say them at all, but they were afraid to proceed to such lengths as that, lest they might call down a sudden and special thunderbolt from heaven. Then at once they reached and hovered upon the verge of sleep—but an intruder came, now, that would not go away. They began to feel a vague fear that they had been doing wrong to run away; and next they thought of the stolen meat, and then the real torture came. They tried to argue it away by reminding themselves that they had stolen sweetmeats and apples scores of times. **SWEETMEATS are candy or sweetened fruit treats. Mmm, they sound good to me!** It seemed to them, in the end, that there was no getting around the stubborn fact that taking sweetmeats was only "hooking," while taking bacon and hams and such valuables was plain simple *stealing*—and there was a command against that in the Bible. So they inwardly resolved that so long as they remained in the business, their piracies should not again be sullied with the crime of stealing. Then these curiously inconsistent pirates fell peacefully to sleep.

10
Camp-Life

When Tom awoke in the morning, he wondered where he was. He sat up and rubbed his eyes and looked around. Then he understood.

It was the cool gray dawn, and there was a delicious sense of peace in the deep silence of the woods.

Tom stirred up the other pirates and they all clattered away with a shout, and in a minute or two were stripped and chasing after and tumbling over each other in the shallow clear water of the white sand-bar. They felt no longing for the little village sleeping in the distance beyond the majestic waste of water. A vagrant current or a slight rise in the river had carried off their raft, but this only gratified them, since its going was something like burning the bridge between them and civilization.

They came back to camp wonderfully refreshed, glad-hearted, and very hungry; and soon they had the camp-fire blazing up again. Huck found a spring of clear cold water close by, and the boys made cups of broad oak or hickory leaves, and felt that water, sweetened with such a wild-wood charm as that, would be a good enough substitute for coffee. While Joe was slicing bacon for breakfast, Tom and Huck asked him to hold on a minute; they stepped to a promising nook in the river bank and threw in their lines; almost immediately they had reward. Joe had not had time to get impatient before they were back again with some handsome bass, a couple of sun-perch and a small catfish—provisions enough for quite a family. They fried the fish with the bacon and were astonished; for no fish had ever seemed so delicious before. They did not know that the quicker a fresh water fish is on the fire after he is caught the better he is; and they reflected little upon what a sauce open air sleeping, open air exercise, bathing, and a large ingredient of hunger makes, too.

Reading about their meal is making me hungry! I'm going to have to find some pirate provisions around here!

They lay around in the shade, after breakfast, while Huck had a smoke, and then went off through the woods on an exploring expedition. They tramped gaily along, over decaying logs, through tangled under-brush. Now and then they came upon snug nooks carpeted with grass and jeweled with flowers.

They found plenty of things to be delighted with, but nothing to be astonished at. They discovered that the island was about three miles long and a quarter of a mile wide, and that the shore it lay closest to was only separated from it by a narrow channel hardly two hundred yards wide. They took a swim about every hour, so it was close upon the middle of the afternoon when they got back to camp. They were too hungry to stop to fish, but they fared sumptuously upon cold ham, and then threw themselves down in the shade to talk. But the talk soon began to drag, and then died. The stillness, the solemnity that brooded in the woods, and the sense of loneliness, began to tell upon the spirits of the boys. They fell to thinking. A sort of undefined longing crept upon them. This took dim shape, presently—it was budding home-sickness. Even Huck was dreaming of his door-steps and empty hogsheads. But they were all ashamed of their weakness, and none was brave enough to speak his thought.

For some time, now, the boys had been dully conscious of a peculiar sound in the distance, just as one sometimes is of the ticking of a clock which he takes no distinct note of. But now this mysterious sound became more pronounced, and forced a recognition. The boys started, glanced at each other, and then each assumed a listening attitude. There was a long silence, profound and unbroken; then a deep, sullen boom came floating down out of the distance.

"What is it!" exclaimed Joe, under his breath.

"I wonder," said Tom in a whisper.

"Tain't thunder," said Huckleberry, in an awed tone, "becuz thunder— "

"Hark!" said Tom. "Listen—don't talk."

They waited a time that seemed an age, and then the same muffled boom troubled the solemn hush.

"Let's go and see."

They sprang to their feet and hurried to the shore toward the town. They parted the bushes on the bank and peered out over the water. The little steam ferry boat was about a mile below the village, drifting with the current. Her broad deck seemed crowded with people. There were a great many skiffs rowing about or floating with the stream in the neighborhood of the ferry boat, but the boys could not determine what the men in them were doing. **A SKIFF is a small boat.** Presently a great jet of white smoke burst from the ferry boat's side, and as it expanded and rose in a lazy cloud, that same dull throb of sound was borne to the listeners again.

"I know now!" exclaimed Tom; "somebody's drownded!"

"That's it!" said Huck; "they done that last summer, when Bill Turner got drownded; they shoot a cannon over the water, and that makes him come up to the top. Yes, and they take loaves of bread and put quicksilver in 'em and set 'em afloat, and wherever there's anybody's that's drownded, they'll float right there and stop."

Quicksilver is mercury. The villagers believe that a loaf of bread with quicksilver in it will draw a dead body to the surface of the water.

"Yes, I've heard about that," said Joe. "I wonder what makes the bread do that."

"Oh, it ain't the bread so much," said Tom; "I reckon it's mostly what they say over it before they start it out."

"But they don't say anything over it," said Huck. "I've seen 'em and they don't."

"Well that's funny," said Tom. "But maybe they say it to themselves. Of *course* they do. Anybody might know that."

The other boys agreed that there was reason in what Tom said, because an ignorant lump of bread, uninstructed by an incantation, could not be expected to act very intelligently when sent upon an errand of such seriousness. **Back in the old days, people believed that an incantation, or magic spell, could make a piece of bread "find" a dead body in the water. This is another example of a superstition. Hey, stranger things have happened!**

"By jings I wish I was over there now," said Joe.

"I do too," said Huck. "I'd give heaps to know who it is."

The boys still listened and watched. Presently a revealing thought flashed through Tom's mind, and he exclaimed:

"Boys, I know who's drownded—it's us!"

They felt like heroes in an instant. Here was a gorgeous triumph; they were missed; they were mourned; hearts were breaking on their account; tears were being shed; accusing memories of unkindnesses to these poor lost lads were rising up; and best of all, the departed were the talk of the whole town, and the envy of all the boys, as far as this dazzling notoriety was concerned. This was fine. It was worth while to be a pirate, after all.

As twilight drew on, the ferry boat went back to her accustomed business and the skiffs disappeared. The pirates returned to camp. They were joyful with vanity over their new grandeur and the trouble they were making. They caught fish, cooked supper and ate it, and then fell to guessing at what the village was thinking and saying about them. But when the shadows of night closed them in, they gradually ceased to talk, and sat gazing into the fire, with their minds evidently wandering elsewhere. The excitement was gone, now, and Tom and Joe could not keep back thoughts of certain persons at home who were not enjoying this fine frolic as much as they were.

As the night deepened, Huck began to nod, and presently to snore. Joe followed next. Tom lay upon his elbow motionless, for some time, watching the two intently. At last he got up cautiously, on his knees, and went searching among the grass and the flickering reflections flung by the camp-fire. He picked up and inspected several large semi-cylinders of the thin white bark of a sycamore, and finally chose one which seemed to suit him. Then he knelt by the fire and painfully wrote something upon the bark with his "red keel," rolled it up, and put it in his jacket pocket. Then he tip-toed his way cautiously among the trees till he felt that he was out of hearing, and straightway broke into a keen run in the direction of the sand-bar.

Even though Tom feels like a hero, he knows Aunt Polly must be worried. After all, the whole town thinks the boys have drowned! So Tom comes up with a plan. He writes a note to his aunt on a piece of bark that says "We ain't dead—we are only off being pirates." His plan is to take the note to his house for Aunt Polly to find. But that won't be easy. He has to cross the river, sneak on board the ferry, and make his way through town in the dark, all without being seen. Then, when he finally gets to Aunt Polly's, he overhears something very interesting. . . .

11
Tom Reveals a Secret

As Tom approaches Aunt Polly's house, he hears voices. He decides to sneak into the house to investigate. Tom overhears Aunt Polly and Joe's mother, Mrs. Harper. They are crying because they believe the boys have drowned, and they feel guilty for not being nice to them when they were "alive." They say how, if only their boys could come back, they would never be mean or punish Tom and Joe again. And that gives Tom another grand idea. He decides not to leave the note, then sneaks out of the house and makes his way back to Jackson's Island and the pirate gang.

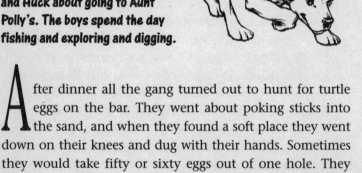

Tom decides not to tell Joe and Huck about going to Aunt Polly's. The boys spend the day fishing and exploring and digging.

After dinner all the gang turned out to hunt for turtle eggs on the bar. They went about poking sticks into the sand, and when they found a soft place they went down on their knees and dug with their hands. Sometimes they would take fifty or sixty eggs out of one hole. They were perfectly round white things. They had a famous fried-egg feast that night, and another on Friday morning.

After breakfast they went whooping and prancing out of the bar, and chased each other round and round, shedding clothes as they went, until they were naked, and then continued the frolic far away up the shallow water of the bar, against the stiff current, which latter tripped their legs from under them from time to time and greatly increased the fun. And now and then they stopped in a group and splashed water in each other's faces with their palms, gradually approaching each other, with averted faces to avoid the strangling sprays and finally gripping and struggling till the best man ducked his neighbor, and then they all went under in a tangle of white legs and arms and came up blowing, sputtering, laughing and gasping for breath at one and the same time.

When they were well exhausted, they would run out and sprawl on the hot sand, and lie there and cover themselves up with it, and by and by break for the water again and go through the original performance once more. Finally it occurred to them that their naked skin represented flesh-colored "tights" very fairly; so they drew a ring in the sand and had a circus—with three clowns in it, for none would yield this proudest post to his neighbor.

Next they got their marbles and played "knucks" and "ring-taw" and "keeps" till that amusement grew stale. Then Joe and Huck had another swim, but Tom would not venture, because he found that in kicking off his trousers he had kicked his rattlesnake rattles off his ankle, and he wondered how he had escaped cramp so long without the protection of this mysterious charm. **In case you couldn't tell, Tom is a pretty superstitious kid.** He did not venture again until he had found it, and by that time the other boys were tired and ready to rest. They gradually wandered apart, dropped into the "dumps," and fell to gazing longingly across the wide river to where the village lay drowsing in the sun. Tom found himself writing "BECKY" in the sand with his big toe; he scratched it out, and was angry with himself for his weakness. But he wrote it again, nevertheless; he could not help it. He erased it once more and then took himself out of temptation by driving the other boys together and joining them.

But Joe's spirit had gone down almost beyond resurrection. He was so homesick that he could hardly endure the misery of it. The tears lay very near the surface. Huck was melancholy, too. Tom was down-hearted, but tried hard not to show it. He had a secret which he was not ready to tell, yet, but if this depression was not broken up soon he would have to bring it out. He said, with a great show of cheerfulness:

"I bet there's been pirates on this island before, boys. We'll explore it again. They've hid treasures here somewhere. How'd you feel to light on a rotten chest full of gold and silver—hey?"

But it roused only a faint enthusiasm, which faded out, with no reply. Tom tried one or two other seductions; but they failed, too. It was discouraging work. Joe sat poking up the sand with a stick and looking very gloomy. Finally he said:

"O, boys, let's give it up. I want to go home. It's so lonesome."

"Oh, no, Joe, you'll feel better by and by," said Tom. "Just think of the fishing that's here."

"I don't care for fishing. I want to go home."

"But Joe, there ain't such another swimming place anywhere."

"Swimming's no good. I don't seem to care for it, somehow, when there ain't anybody to say I shan't go in. I mean to go home."

"O, shucks! Baby! You want to see your mother, I reckon."

"Yes, I *do* want to see my mother—and you would, too, if you had one. I ain't any more baby than you are." And Joe snuffled a little.

"Well, we'll let the cry-baby go home to his mother, *won't* we Huck? Poor thing—does it want to see its mother? And so it shall. *You* like it here, *don't* you Huck? We'll stay, won't we?"

Huck said "Y-e-s"—without any heart in it.

"I'll never speak to you again as long as I live," said Joe, rising. "There now!" And he moved moodily away and began to dress himself.

"Who cares!" said Tom. "Nobody wants you to. Go 'long home and get laughed at. O, you're a nice pirate. Huck and me ain't cry-babies. We'll stay, won't we Huck? Let him go if he wants to. I reckon we can get along without him, per'aps."

But Tom was uneasy, nevertheless, and was alarmed to see Joe go sullenly on with his dressing. And then it was discomforting to see Huck eyeing Joe's preparations so longingly. Presently, without a parting word, Joe began to wade off toward the Illinois shore. Tom's heart began to sink. He glanced at Huck. Huck could not bear the look, and dropped his eyes. Then he said:

"I want to go, too, Tom. It was getting so lonesome, anyway, and now it'll be worse. Let's us go, too, Tom."

"I won't! You can all go, if you want to. I mean to stay."

"Tom, I better go."

"Well, go 'long—who's hendering you."

Huck began to pick up his scattered clothes. He said:

"Tom, I wisht you'd come, too. Now, you think it over. We'll wait for you when we get to shore."

"Well, you'll wait a blame long time, that's all."

Huck started sorrowfully away, and Tom stood looking after him, with a strong desire tugging at his heart to yield his pride, and go along, too. He hoped the boys would stop, but they still waded slowly on. It suddenly dawned on Tom that it was become very lonely and still. He made one final struggle with his pride, and then darted after his comrades, yelling:

"Wait! Wait! I want to tell you something!"

They presently stopped and turned around. When he got to where they were, he began unfolding his secret, and they listened moodily till at last they saw the "point" he was driving at, and then they set up a war-whoop of applause, and said it was "splendid!" and said if he had told them at first, they wouldn't have started away. He made a plausible excuse; but his real reason had been the fear that not even the secret would keep them with him any very great length of time, and so he had meant to hold it in reserve as a last temptation.

Tom has finally revealed his grand plan to his fellow pirates—the plan he came up with at Aunt Polly's. But what is it? What is it?

About midnight Joe awoke, and called the boys. There was a brooding oppressiveness in the air that seemed to foretell something. The boys huddled themselves together and sought the friendly companionship of the fire, though the dull dead heat of the breathless atmosphere was stifling.

They sat still, intent and waiting. The solemn hush continued. Beyond the light of the fire everything was swallowed up in the blackness of darkness. Presently there came a quivering glow that vaguely revealed the foliage for a moment and then vanished. By and by another came, a little stronger. Then another. Then a faint moan came sighing through the branches of the forest and the boys felt a fleeting breath upon their cheeks, and shuddered with the idea that the Spirit of the Night had gone by. There was a pause. Now a weird flash turned night into day and showed every little grass-blade, separate and distinct, that grew about their feet. And it showed three white, startled faces, too. A deep peal of thunder went rolling and tumbling down the heavens and lost itself in sullen rumblings in the distance. A sweep of chilly air passed by, rustling all the leaves and snowing the flaky ashes about the fire. Another fierce flare lit up the forest and an instant crash followed that seem to tear the tree-tops right over the boys' heads. They clung together in terror, in the thick gloom that followed. A few big raindrops fell pattering upon the leaves.

"Quick! boys, go for the tent!" exclaimed Tom.

They sprang away, stumbling over roots and among vines in the dark, no two plunging in the same direction. A furious blast roared through the trees, making everything sing as it went. One blinding flash after another came, and peal on peal of deafening thunder. And now a drenching rain poured down and the rising hurricane drove it in sheets along the ground. The boys cried out to each other, but the roaring wind and the booming thunder-blasts drowned their voices utterly. However one by one they straggled in at last and took shelter under the tent, cold, scared and streaming with water; but to have company in misery seemed something to be grateful for. They could not talk, the old sail flapped so furiously, even if the other noises would have allowed them. The tempest rose higher and higher, and presently the sail tore loose from its fastenings and went winging away on the blast. The boys seized each others' hands and fled, with many tumblings and bruises to the shelter of a great oak that stood upon the river bank. Now the battle was at its highest. The unflagging thunder-peals came now in ear-splitting explosive bursts, keen and sharp, and unspeakably appalling. The storm culminated in one matchless effort that seemed likely to tear the island to pieces, burn it up, drown it to the tree tops, blow it away, and deafen every creature in it, all at one and the same moment. It was a wild night for homeless young heads to be out in.

But at last the battle was done, and the forces retired with weaker and weaker threatenings and grumblings, and peace resumed. The boys went back to camp, a good deal awed; but they found there was still something to be thankful for, because the great sycamore, the shelter of their beds, was a ruin, now, blasted by the lightnings, and they were not under it when the catastrophe happened.

Everything in camp was drenched, the camp-fire as well; for they had made no provision against rain. Here was matter for dismay, for they were soaked through and chilled. They were eloquent in their distress; but they presently discovered that their fire had eaten so far up under the great log it had been built against that a hand-breath or so of it had escaped wetting; so they patiently worked until, with shreds and bark gathered from the under sides of sheltered logs, they coaxed the fire to burn again. Then they piled on great dead boughs till they had a roaring furnace and were glad-hearted once more. They dried their boiled ham and had a feast, and after that they sat by the fire and expanded and glorified their midnight adventure until morning, for there was not a dry spot to sleep on, anywhere around.

We will leave them to chatter and brag, since we have no further use for them at present.

12
Memories of the Lost Heroes

Meanwhile, back at the village, it is Sunday morning. Aunt Polly is grieving for her Tom and the entire village is preparing for the funeral for Tom, Joe, and Huck.

When the Sunday-school hour was finished, the bell began to toll, instead of ringing in the usual way. The villagers began to gather, loitering a moment in the vestibule to converse in whispers about the sad event. But there was no whispering in the church itself; only the rustling of dresses, as the women gathered to their seats, disturbed the silence there. None could remember when the little church had been so full before. There was finally a waiting pause. Then Aunt Polly entered, followed by Sid and Mary, and they by the Harper family, all in deep black, and the whole congregation, the old minister as well, rose reverently and stood, until the mourners were seated in the front pew. There was another communing silence, broken by muffled sobs, and then the minister spread his hands abroad and prayed. A moving hymn was sung, and the text followed: "I am the Resurrection and the Life."

The minister related many a touching incident in the lives of the departed, which illustrated their sweet, generous natures, and the people could easily see, now, how noble and beautiful those episodes were, and remembered with grief that at the time they occurred they had seemed completely bad, well deserving of the cowhide. **Deserving of the cowhide means they deserved to be whipped.** The congregation became more and more moved, as the pathetic tale went on, till at last the whole company broke down and joined the weeping mourners in a chorus of anguished sobs, the preacher himself giving way to his feelings, and crying in the pulpit.

There was a rustle in the gallery, which nobody noticed; a moment later the church door creaked; the minister raised his streaming eyes above his handkerchief, and stood transfixed! First one and then another pair of eyes followed the minister's, and then almost with one impulse the congregation rose and stared while the three dead boys come marching up the aisle, Tom in the lead, Joe next, and Huck, a ruin of drooping rags, sneaking sheepishly in the rear! They had been hid in the unused gallery listening to their own funeral sermon!

Aunt Polly, Mary and the Harpers threw themselves upon their restored ones, smothered them with kisses and poured out thanksgivings, while poor Huck stood embarrassed and uncomfortable, not knowing exactly what to do or where to hide from so many unwelcoming eyes. He wavered, and started to slink away, but Tom seized him and said:

"Aunt Polly, it ain't fair. Somebody's got to be glad to see Huck."

"And so they shall. I'm glad to see him, poor

motherless thing!" And the loving attentions Aunt Polly lavished upon him were the one thing capable of making him more uncomfortable than he was before.

Suddenly the minister shouted at the top of his voice:

"Praise God from whom all blessings flow—SING!—and put your hearts in it!"

And they did. The song swelled up with a triumphant burst, and while it shook the rafters Tom Sawyer the Pirate looked around upon the envying juveniles about him and confessed in his heart that this was the proudest moment of his life.

13
Muff Potter in Court

That was Tom's great secret — to return home with his fellow pirates to attend their own funeral. A few days later, Tom's class let out for summer, and Becky left St. Petersburg for a vacation in Constantinople. Everyone is enjoying the lazy summer days. But something important is on Tom's mind—Muff Potter's trial. Remember, Muff Potter is on trial for murdering Dr. Robinson. Tom and Huck have to keep the big secret of who the real murderer is: Injun Joe!

A t last the murder trial came on in the court. It became the absorbing topic of village talk immediately. Tom could not get away from it. Every reference to the murder sent a shudder to his heart. It kept him in a cold shiver all the time. He took Huck to a lonely place to have a talk with him. It would be some relief to unseal his tongue for a little while; to divide his burden of distress with another sufferer. Moreover, he wanted to assure himself that Huck had remained discreet.

"Huck, have you ever told anybody about—that?"

" 'Bout what?"

"You know what."

"Oh—'course I haven't."

"Never a word?"

"Never a solitary word, so help me. What makes you ask?"

"Well, I was afeard."

"Why Tom Sawyer, we wouldn't be alive two days if that got found out. *You* know that."

Tom felt more comfortable. After a pause:

"Huck, they couldn't anybody get you to tell, could they?"

"Get me to tell? Why if I wanted that half-breed devil to drown me they could get me to tell. They ain't no different way."

"Well, that's all right, then. I reckon we're safe as long as we keep mum. But let's swear again, anyway. It's more surer."

"I'm agreed."

So they swore again with dread.

"What is the talk around, Huck? I've heard a power of it."

"Talk? Well, it's just Muff Potter, Muff Potter, Muff Potter all the time. It keeps me in a sweat, constant, so's I want to hide som'ers."

"That's just the same way they go on round me. I reckon he's a goner. Don't you feel sorry for him, sometimes?"

"Most always—most always. He ain't no account; but then he hain't ever done anything to hurt anybody. Just fishes a little, to get money to get drunk on—and loafs around considerable; but lord we all do that—leastways most of us. But he's kind of good—he give me half a fish once, when there warn't enough for two; and lots of times he's kind of stood by me when I was out of luck."

"Well, he's mended kites for me, Huck, and knitted hooks on to my line. I wish we could get him out of there."

"My! we couldn't get him out Tom. And besides, 'twouldn't do any good; they'd ketch him again."

"Yes—so they would. But I hate to hear 'em abuse him so like the dickens when he never done—that."

"I do too, Tom. Lord, I hear 'em say he's the bloodiest looking villain in this country, and they wonder he wasn't ever hung before."

"Yes, they talk like that, all the time. I've heard 'em say that if he was to get free they'd lynch him."

To lynch is to punish a person for a crime, usually by hanging them, without allowing the person a fair trial. This was a common practice back then.

"And they'd do it, too."

The boys had a long talk, but it brought them little comfort. As the twilight drew on, they found themselves hanging about the neighborhood of the little isolated jail, perhaps with an undefined hope that something would happen that might clear away their difficulties. But nothing happened; there seemed to be no angels or fairies interested in this luckless captive.

The boys did as they had often done before—went to the cell grating and gave Potter some tobacco and matches. He was on the ground floor and there were no guards.

Helllooo! Start flipping the pages and check out the action.... Woo-cha!

His gratitude for their gifts had always struck their consciences before—it cut deeper than ever, this time. They felt cowardly and treacherous to the last degree when Potter said:

"You've been mighty good to me, boys—better'n anybody else in this town. And I don't forget it, I don't. Often I says to myself, says I, 'I used to mend all the boys' kites and things, and show 'em where the good fishin' places was, and befriend 'em what I could, and now they've all forgot old Muff when he's in trouble; but Tom don't, and Huck don't—*they* don't forget him,' says I, 'and I don't forget them.' Well, boys, I done an awful thing—drunk and crazy at the time—that's the only way I account for it—and now I got to swing for it, and it's right. Right, and *best*, too I reckon—hope so, anyway. Well, we won't talk about that. I don't want to make *you* feel bad; you've befriended me. But what I want to say, is, don't *you* ever get drunk—then you won't ever get here. Stand a little furder west—so—that's it; it's a prime comfort to see faces that's friendly when a body's in such a muck of trouble, and there don't none come here but yourn. Good friendly faces—good friendly faces. Git up on one another's backs and let me touch 'em. That's it. Shake hands—yourn'll come through the bars, but mine's too big. Little hands, and weak—but they've helped Muff Potter a power, and they'd help him more if they could."

Tom went home miserable, and his dreams that night were full of horrors. The next day and the day after, he hung about the court-room, drawn by an almost irresistible impulse to go in, but forcing himself to stay out. Huck was having the same experience. They studiously avoided each other. Each wandered away, from time to time, but the same dismal fascination always brought them back presently. Tom kept his ears open when people strolled out of the court-room, but invariably heard distressing news. At the end of the second day the village talk was to the effect that Injun Joe's evidence stood firm and unshaken, and that there was not the slightest question as to what the jury's verdict would be.

Tom was out late, that night, and came to bed through the window. He was in a tremendous state of excitement. It was hours before he got to sleep. All the village flocked to the court-house the next morning, for this was to be the great day. After a long wait the jury filed in and took their places; shortly afterward, Potter, pale and haggard, timid and hopeless, was brought in, with chains upon him, and seated where all the curious eyes could stare at him; no less obvious was Injun Joe, stolid as ever. There was another pause, and then the judge arrived and the sheriff proclaimed the opening of the court. The usual whisperings among the lawyers and gathering together of papers followed.

Now a witness was called who testified that he found Muff Potter washing in the brook, at an early hour of the morning that the murder was discovered, and that he immediately sneaked away. After some further questioning counsel for the prosecution said:

"Take the witness."

In this trial, the prosecution is trying to show that Muff is guilty. The defense will try to show that Muff, the defendant, is not guilty. Muff knows that if he is found guilty he will die. So he is counting on the defense to prove his innocence.

The prisoner raised his eyes for a moment, but dropped them again when his own counsel said:

"I have no questions to ask him."

The next witness proved the finding of the knife near the corpse. Counsel for the prosecution said:

"Take the witness."

"I have no questions to ask him," Potter's lawyer replied.

A third witness swore he had often seen the knife in Potter's possession.

"Take the witness."

Counsel for Potter declined to question him. The faces of the audience began to betray annoyance. Did this attorney mean to throw away his client's life without an effort?

Several witnesses spoke concerning Potter's guilty behavior when brought to the scene of the murder. They were allowed to leave the stand without being cross-questioned.

Every detail of the damaging circumstances that occurred in the graveyard upon that morning which all present remembered so well, was brought out by credible witnesses, but none of them were cross-examined by Potter's lawyer. Counsel for the prosecution now said:

"By the oaths of citizens whose simple word is above suspicion, we have tied this awful crime beyond all possibility of question, upon this unhappy prisoner. We rest our case here."

A groan escaped from poor Potter, and he put his face in his hands and rocked his body softly to and fro, while a painful silence reigned in the court-room. Many men were moved, and many women's compassion testified itself in tears. Counsel for the defence rose and said:

"Your honor, in our remarks at the opening of this trial, we told you of our purpose to prove that our client did this fearful deed while under the influence of a blind and irresponsible confusion produced by drink. We have changed our mind. We shall not offer that plea." [Then to the clerk]: "Call Thomas Sawyer."

A puzzled amazement awoke in every face in the house. Every eye fastened itself with wondering interest upon Tom as he rose and took his place upon the stand. The boy looked wild enough, for he was badly scared. The oath was administered.

"Thomas Sawyer, where were you on the seventeenth of June, about the hour of midnight?"

Tom glanced at Injun Joe's iron face and his tongue failed him. The audience listened breathless, but the words refused to come. After a few moments, however, the boy got a little of his strength back, and managed to put enough of it into his voice to make part of the house hear:

"In the graveyard!"

"A little bit louder, please. Don't be afraid. You were—"

"In the graveyard."

A mocking smile flitted across Injun Joe's face.

"Were you anywhere near Horse Williams's grave?"

"Yes, sir."

"Speak up—just a trifle louder. How near were you?"

"Near as I am to you."

"Were you hidden, or not?"

"I was hid."

"Where?"

"Behind the elms that's on the edge of the grave."

Injun Joe gave a barely perceptible start.

"Any one with you?"

"Yes, sir. I went there with—"

"Wait—wait a moment. Never mind mentioning your companion's name. We will produce him at the proper time.

Did you carry anything there with you?" Tom hesitated and looked confused.

"Speak out my boy. The truth is always respectable. What did you take there?"

"Only a—a—dead cat."

There was a ripple of laughter, which the court checked.

"We will produce the skeleton of that cat. Now my boy, tell us everything that occurred—tell it in your own way—don't skip anything, and don't be afraid."

Tom began—hesitatingly at first, but as he warmed to his subject his words flowed more and more easily; in a little while every sound ceased but his own voice; every eye fixed itself upon him; with parted lips and bated breath the audience hung upon his words, taking no note of time, rapt in the ghastly fascinations of the tale. The strain upon pent emotion reached its climax when the boy said—

"—and as the doctor fetched the board around and Muff Potter fell, Injun Joe jumped with the knife and—"

Crash! Quick as lightning the half-breed sprang for a window, tore his way through all opposers, and was gone!

Injun Joe has escaped! He jumped through the courthouse window to avoid capture! Now the whole town knows that Muff Potter is innocent. Tom is a hero, but you can bet that Injun Joe will be looking to settle the score. What will Tom and Huck do now?

14
Search for the Treasure

As you can imagine, Tom and Huck lived in constant terror. They thought at any moment Injun Joe would suddenly appear to get his revenge. The days weren't so bad, but the nights were awful. But time went on, and no one spotted Injun Joe, so eventually the boys put 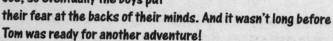 their fear at the backs of their minds. And it wasn't long before Tom was ready for another adventure!

There comes a time in every boy's life when he has a raging desire to go somewhere and dig for hidden treasure. This desire suddenly came upon Tom one day. He set out to find Joe Harper, but failed of success. Next he sought Ben Rogers; he had gone fishing. Presently he stumbled upon Huck Finn. Huck would answer. Tom took him to a private place and opened the matter to him confidentially. Huck was willing.

"Where'll we dig?" said Huck.

"O, most anywhere."

"Why, is it hid all around?"

"No indeed it ain't. It's hid in mighty particular places, Huck—sometimes on islands, sometimes in rotten chests under the end of a limb of an old dead tree, just where the shadow falls at midnight; but mostly under the floor in ha'nted houses."

"Who hides it?"

"Why robbers, of course—who'd you reckon? Sunday-school sup'rintendents?"

"I don't know. If 'twas mine I wouldn't hide it; I'd spend it and have a good time."

"So would I. But robbers don't do that way. They always hide it and leave it there."

It makes sense to me. I always bury my most treasured items—bones.

"Don't they come after it any more?"

"No, they think they will, but they generally forget the marks, or else they die. Anyway, it lays there a long time and gets rusty; and by and by somebody finds an old yellow paper that tells how to find the marks.

"Have you got one of them papers, Tom?"

"No."

"Well then, how you going to find the marks?"

"I don't want any marks. They always bury it under a ha'nted house or on an island, or under a dead tree that's got one limb sticking out. Well, we've tried Jackson's Island a little, and we can try it again some time; and there's the old ha'nted house up the Still-House branch, and there's lots of dead-limb trees—dead loads of 'em."

"Is it under all of them?"

"How you talk! No!"

"Then how you going to know which one to go for?"

"Go for all of 'em!"

"Why Tom, it'll take all summer."

"Well, what of that? Suppose you find a brass pot with

a hundred dollars in it, all rusty and gray, or a rotten chest full of di'monds. How's that?"

Huck's eyes glowed.

"That's bully. Plenty bully enough for me. Just you gimme the hundred dollars and I don't want no di'monds."

"All right. But I bet you *I* ain't going to throw off on di'monds. Some of 'em's worth twenty dollars apiece—there ain't any, hardly, but what's worth six bits or a dollar."

"No! Is that so?"

"Cert'nly—anybody'll tell you so. Hain't you ever seen one, Huck?"

"Not as I remember."

"O, kings have slathers of them."

"Well, I don't know no kings, Tom."

"I reckon you don't. But if you was to go to Europe you'd see a raft of 'em hopping around."

"Do they hop?"

"Hop?—your granny! No!"

"Well what did you say they did, for?"

"Shucks, I only meant you'd *see* 'em—not hopping, of course—what do they want to hop for?—but I mean you'd just see 'em—scattered around, you know, in a kind of a general way."

"But say—where you going to dig first?"

"Well I don't know. S'pose we tackle that old dead-limb tree on the hill t'other side of Still-House branch?"

"I'm agreed."

So they got a crippled pick and a shovel, and set out on their three-mile tramp. They arrived hot and panting, and threw themselves down in the shade of a neighboring elm to rest and have a smoke.

"I like this," said Tom.

"So do I."

They worked and sweated for half an hour. No result. They toiled another half hour. Still no result. Huck said:

"Do they always bury it as deep as this?"

"Sometimes—not always. Not generally. I reckon we haven't got the right place."

"Where you going to dig next, after we get this one?"

"I reckon maybe we'll tackle the old tree that's over yonder on Cardiff Hill back of the widow's."

"I reckon that'll be a good one. But won't the widow take it away from us Tom? It's on her land."

"*She* take it away! Maybe she'd like to try it once. Whoever finds one of these hid treasures, it belongs to him. It don't make any difference whose land it's on."

That was satisfactory. The work went on. By and by Huck said:

"Blame it, we must be in the wrong place again. What do you think?"

"It *is* mighty curious, Huck. I don't understand it. Sometimes witches interfere. I reckon maybe that's what's the trouble now."

"Shucks, witches ain't got no power in the daytime."

"Well, that's so. I didn't think of that."

"Say, Tom, let's give this place up, and try somewheres else."

"All right, I reckon we better."

"Whar'll it be?"

Tom considered a while; and then said:

"The ha'nted house. That's it!"

"Blame it, I don't like ha'nted houses, Tom. Why they're a dern sight worse'n dead people. Dead people might talk, maybe, but they don't come sliding around when you ain't noticing, and peep over your shoulder all of a sudden and grit their teeth, the way a ghost does. I couldn't stand such a thing as that, Tom—nobody could."

"Yes, but Huck, ghosts don't travel around only at night. They won't hender us from digging there in the day time."

"Well, all right. We'll tackle the ha'nted house if you say so—but I reckon it's taking chances."

They had started down the hill by this time. There in the middle of the moonlit valley below them stood the "ha'nted" house, utterly isolated, its fences gone long ago, rank weed smothering the very doorsteps, the chimney crumbled to ruin, the window-sashes vacant, a corner of the roof caved in. The boys gazed a while, half expecting to see a ghost flit past a window; then talking in a low tone, as befitted the time and the circumstances, they struck far off to the right, to give the haunted house a wide berth, and took their way homeward through the woods that adorned the rearward side of Cardiff Hill.

Tom and Huck decided to investigate the haunted house during the daylight and not at night. I don't blame them. I mean, it's not that I'm AFRAID of ghosts . . . I just, um . . . respect them. Yeah, that's it.

15

The Haunted House

The next day was Friday, and Tom and Huck took a break from hunting for treasure and played Robin Hood. Then Saturday morning dawned, and the dedicated treasure hunters were going back to work.

O n Saturday, shortly after noon, the boys were at the dead tree again. They had a smoke and a chat in the shade, and then dug a little in their last hole, not with great hope, but merely because Tom said there were so many cases where people had given up a treasure after getting down within six inches of it, and then somebody else had come along and turned it up with a single thrust of a shovel. The thing failed this time, however, so the boys shouldered their tools and went away.

When they reached the haunted house there was something so weird and grisly about the dead silence that reigned there under the baking sun, and something so depressing about the loneliness and desolation of the place, that they were afraid, for a moment, to venture in. Then they crept to the door and took a trembling peep. They saw a weed-grown, floorless room, unplastered, an ancient fireplace, vacant windows, a ruinous staircase; and here, there, and everywhere, hung ragged and abandoned cobwebs. They presently entered, softly, with quickened

pulses,
talking in
whispers,
ears alert to
catch the slightest
sound, and muscles
tense and ready for
instant retreat.

In a little while familiarity lessened their fears and they gave the place a critical and interested examination, rather admiring their own bravery, and wondering at it, too.

Next they wanted to look upstairs. This was something like cutting off retreat, but they got to daring each other, and of course there could be but one result—they threw their tools into a corner and made the ascent. Up there were the same signs of decay. In one corner they found a closet that promised mystery, but the promise was a fraud—there was nothing in it. Their courage was up now and well in hand. They were about to go down and begin work when—

"Sh!" said Tom.

"What is it?" whispered Huck, blanching with fright.

"Sh! . . . . . There! . . . . . Hear it?"

"Yes! . . . . . O, my! Let's run!"

"Keep still! Don't you budge! They're coming right toward the door."

The boys stretched themselves upon the floor with their eyes to knot holes in the planking, and lay waiting, in a misery of fear.

"They've stopped . . . . . No—coming . . . . . Here they are. Don't whisper another word, Huck. My goodness, I wish I was out of this!"

Two men entered. Each boy said to himself: "There's the old deaf and dumb Spaniard that's been about town once or twice lately—never saw t'other man before."

"T'other" was a ragged, unkempt creature, with nothing very pleasant in his face. The Spaniard was wrapped in a *serape*; he had bushy white whiskers; long white hair flowed from under his sombrero, and he wore green goggles. When they came in, "t'other" was talking in a low voice; they sat

> "Serape" is a Spanish word for a blanket that you wear for warmth.

95

down on the ground, facing the door, with their backs to the wall, and the speaker continued his remarks. His manner became less guarded and his words more distinct as he proceeded:

"No," said he, "I've thought it all over, and I don't like it. It's dangerous."

"Dangerous!" grunted the "deaf and dumb" Spaniard—to the vast surprise of the boys.

This voice made the boys gasp and quake. It was Injun Joe's! **So Injun Joe has been in town all along, dressed in disguise as the "deaf and dumb" Spaniard.** There was silence for some time.

Then Joe said:

"Well, what's more dangerous than coming here in the day time!—anybody would suspicion us that saw us."

"*I* know that. But there warn't any other place as handy after that fool of a job. I want to quit this shanty. I wanted to Thursday, only it warn't any use trying to stir out of here, with those infernal boys playing over there on the hill right in full view."

"Those infernal boys." He quaked again.

Yipes! The boys playing on the hill were Tom and Huck!

The two men got out some food and made a luncheon. After a long and thoughtful silence, Injun Joe said:

"Look here, lad—you go back up the river where you belong. Wait there till you here from me. I'll take the chances on dropping this into town just once more, for a look. We'll do that 'dangerous' job after I've spied around a little and think things look well for it. Then for Texas! We'll leg it together!"

This was satisfactory. Injun Joe said:

"Nearly time for us to be moving, pard. What'll we do with what little swag we've got left?"

Swag is stolen money, goods, or property.

"I don't know—leave it here as we've always done, I reckon. No use to take it away till we start south. Six hundred and fifty in silver's something to carry."

"Well—all right—it won't matter to come here once more."

"No—but I'd say come in the night as we used to do—it's better."

"Yes; but look here; it may be a good while before I get the right chance at that job; accidents might happen; 'tain't in such a very good place; we'll just bury it—and bury it deep."

"Good idea," said the comrade, who walked across the room, knelt down, raised one of the rearward hearthstones and took out a bag that jingled pleasantly. He subtracted from it twenty or thirty dollars for himself and as much for Injun Joe and passed the bag to the latter, who was on his knees in the corner, now, digging with his bowie knife.

The boys forgot all their fears, all their miseries in an instant. With gloating eyes they watched every movement. Luck!—the splendor of it was beyond all imagination! Six hundred dollars was money enough to make half a dozen boys rich! Here was treasure-hunting under the happiest auspices—there would not be any bothersome uncertainty as to where to dig. They nudged each other every moment—eloquent nudges and easily understood, for they simply meant—"O, but ain't you glad *now* we're here!"

Joe's knife struck upon something.

"Hello!" he said.

"What is it?" said his comrade.

"Half-rotten plank—no it's a box, I believe. Here—bear

a hand and we'll see what it's here for. Never mind, I've broke a hole."

He reached his hand in and drew it out—

"Man, it's money!"

The two men examined the handful of coins. They were gold. The boys above were as excited as themselves, and as delighted.

Joe's comrade said—

"We'll make quick work of this. There's an old rusty pick over amongst the weeds in the corner the other side of the fireplace—I saw it a minute ago."

He ran and brought the boy's pick and shovel. Injun Joe took the pick, looked it over critically, shook his head, muttered something to himself, and then began to use it. The box was soon unearthed. It was not very large; it was iron bound and had been very strong before the slow years had injured it. The men studied the treasure closely a while in blissful silence.

"Pard, there's thousands of dollars here," said Injun Joe.

" 'Twas always said that Murrel's gang cruised around here one summer," the stranger observed.

"I know it," said Injun Joe; "and this looks like it, I should say."

There really was a gang of thieves, led by John A. Murrell, who traveled up and down the Mississippi River. Mark Twain heard stories about these outlaws when he was growing up in Hannibal. He then decided to add them to his book.

"*Now* you won't need to do that job."

The half-breed frowned. Said he—

"You don't know me. Least you don't know all about that thing. 'Taint robbery altogether—it's *revenge*!" and a wicked light flamed in his eyes. "I'll need your help in it. When its finished—then Texas. Go home and stand by till you hear from me."

"Well—if you say so, what'll we do with this—bury it again?"

"Yes. *No!* I'd nearly forgot. That pick had fresh earth on it. [The boys were sick with terror in a moment.] What business has a pick and a shovel here? What business with fresh earth on them? Who brought them here—and where are they gone? Have you heard anybody?—seen anybody? What! bury it again and leave them to come and see the ground disturbed? Not exactly—not exactly. We'll take it to my den."

"Why of course! Might have thought of that before. You mean Number One?"

"No—Number Two—under the cross. The other place is bad—too common."

"All right. It's nearly dark enough to start."

Injun Joe got up and went about from window to window cautiously peeping out. Presently he said:

"Who could have brought these tools here? Do you reckon they can be upstairs?"

The boys' breath left them. Injun Joe put his hand on his knife, halted a moment, undecided, and then turned toward the stairway. The boys thought of the closet, but their strength was gone. The steps came creaking up the stairs. The lads were about to spring for the closet, when there was a crash of rotten timbers and Injun Joe landed on the ground amid the debris of the ruined stairway. He gathered himself up cursing, and his comrade said:

"Now what the use of all that? If it's anybody, and they're up there, let them *stay* there—who cares? If they want to jump down, now, and get into trouble, who objects? It will be dark in fifteen minutes—and then let them follow us if they want to. I'm willing. In my opinion, whoever brought those things in here caught a sight of us and took us for ghosts or devils or something. I'll bet they're running yet."

Joe grumbled a while; then he agreed with his friend that what daylight was left ought to be saved for getting things ready for leaving. Shortly afterward they slipped out of the house in the deepening twilight, and moved toward the river with their precious box.

Tom and Huck rose up, weak but vastly relieved, and stared after them through the chinks between the logs of the house. Follow? Not they. They were content to reach ground again without broken necks, and take the townward track over the hill. They did not talk much. They were too much absorbed in hating themselves—hating the ill luck that made them take the shovel and the pick there. But for that, Injun Joe never would have suspected. He would have hidden the silver with the gold to wait there till his "revenge" was satisfied, and then he would have had the misfortune to find that money turn up missing. Bitter, bitter luck that the tools were ever brought there!

They resolved to keep a lookout for that Spaniard when he should come to town spying out for chances to do his revengeful job, and follow him to "Number Two," wherever that might be. Then a ghastly thought occurred to Tom:

"Revenge? What if he means *us*, Huck?"

"O, don't!" said Huck, nearly fainting.

They talked it all over, and as they entered town they agreed to believe that he might possibly mean somebody else—at least that he might at least mean nobody but Tom, since only Tom had testified.

Very, very small comfort it was to Tom to be alone in danger! Company would be a definite improvement, he thought.

Talk about close calls! Injun Joe suspected something when he saw the pick and shovel. If those stairs hadn't broken . . . ooh, it's too awful to think about! Tom and Huck have had another brush with danger, but you can bet it's not going to stop them from going after that treasure. Read on!

16
The Picnic

Tom and Huck are on the lookout for Injun Joe, hoping he will lead them to the treasure hidden in the secret hiding place, "Number Two." Huck has the night watch, and Tom is supposed to wait at home in case Huck comes with their signal. Meanwhile, Becky has returned from vacation and plans for a big picnic are underway.

The first thing Tom heard on Friday morning was a glad piece of news—Judge Thatcher's family had come back to town the night before. Both Injun Joe and the treasure sunk into secondary importance for a moment, and Becky took the chief place in the boy's interest. He saw her and they had an exhausting good time playing "hi-spy" and "gully-keeper" with a crowd of their schoolmates. The day was completed and crowned in a peculiarly satisfactory way: Becky teased her mother to choose the next day for a picnic, and she consented. **I love picnics . . . but then, I love anything built around eating!** The child's delight was boundless. The invitations were sent out before sunset, and straightway the young folks of the village were thrown into a fever of preparation and pleasurable anticipation. Tom's excitement enabled him to keep awake until a pretty late hour, and he had good hopes of hearing Huck's "meow," and of having his treasure to astonish Becky and the picnickers with, next day; but he was disappointed. No signal came that night.

Morning came, eventually, and by ten or eleven o'clock a giddy and rollicking company were gathered at Judge Thatcher's, and everything was ready for a start. It was not the custom for elderly people to spoil picnics with their presence. The children were considered safe enough under the wings of a few young ladies of eighteen and a few young gentlemen of twenty-three or thereabouts. The old steam ferry-boat was chartered for the occasion; presently the cheerful crowd filed up the main street laden with provision baskets. Sid was sick and had to miss the fun; Mary remained at home to entertain him. The last thing Mrs. Thatcher said to Becky, was—

"You'll not get back till late. Perhaps you'd better stay all night with some of the girls that live near the ferry landing, child."

"Then I'll stay with Susy Harper, mamma."

"Very well. And mind and behave yourself and don't be any trouble."

Presently, as they tripped along, Tom said to Becky:

"Say—I'll tell you what we'll do. 'Stead of going to Joe Harper's we'll climb right up the hill and stop at the Widow Douglas's. She'll have ice cream! She has it most every day— loads of it. And she'll be awful glad to have us." **The Widow Douglas is a kind woman who loves kids. Her house is a favorite hangout for children in the village, mostly because she always seems to have a good supply of ice cream! Hmmm . . . I wonder if she's a dog person, too. . . .**

"O, that will be fun!"

Then Becky reflected a moment and said:

"But what will mamma say?"

"How'll she ever know?"

The girl turned the idea over in her mind, and said reluctantly:

"I reckon it's wrong—but—"

"But shucks! Your mother won't know, and so what's the harm? All she wants is that you'll be safe; and I bet you she'd 'a' said go there if she'd 'a' thought of it. I know she would!"

The widow Douglas's splendid hospitality was a tempting bait. It and Tom's persuasions presently carried the day. So it was decided to say nothing to anybody about the night's programme. Presently it occurred to Tom that maybe Huck might come this very night and give the signal. Still he could not bear to give up the fun at Widow Douglas's. And why should he give it up, he reasoned—the signal did not come the night before, so why should it be any more likely to come tonight? The sure fun of the evening outweighed the uncertain treasure; and boy like, he determined to not allow himself to think of the box of money another time that day.

Three miles below town the ferry-boat stopped at the mouth of a woody hollow and tied up. The crowd swarmed ashore and soon the forest distances and craggy heights echoed far and near with shoutings and laughter. All the different ways of getting hot and tired were gone through with, and by and by wandering children straggled back to camp with responsible appetites, and then the destruction of the good food began. After the feast there was a refreshing season of rest and chat in the shade of spreading oaks. By and by somebody shouted—

"Who's ready for the cave?"

Everybody was. Bundles of candles were gathered, and straightway there was a general scamper up the hill. The mouth of the cave was up the hillside—an opening shaped like a letter A. It's massive oaken door stood unlocked. Within was a small chamber, chilly as an ice-house, and walled by Nature with solid limestone that was dewy with a cold sweat. It was romantic and mysterious to stand here in the deep gloom and look out upon the green valley shining in the sun. But the impressiveness of the situation quickly wore off, and the romping began again. The moment a candle was lighted there was a general rush upon the owner of it; a struggle and a gallant defense followed, but the candle was soon knocked down or blown out, and then there was a glad clamor of laughter and a new chase. But all things have an end. By and by the procession went filing down the steep descent of the main avenue, the flickering rank of lights dimly revealing the lofty walls of rock. This main avenue was not more than eight or ten feet wide. Every few steps other lofty and still narrower crevices branched from it on either hand—for McDougal's cave was but a vast maze of crooked isles that ran into each other and out again and led nowhere. It was said that one might wander days and nights together through its tangle of rifts and chasms, and never find the end of the cave; and that he might go down, and down, and still down, into the earth, and it was just the same—maze underneath maze, and no end to any of them. No man "knew" the cave. That was an impossible thing. Most of the young men knew a portion of it, and it was not customary to venture much beyond this known portion. Tom Sawyer knew as much of the cave as any one. **Ever wonder where caves come from? It's like this: Rainwater drips down through a kind of rock called limestone. It takes thousands of years, but the dripping water finally wears away the rock, and bingo—you've got a cave!**

The procession moved along the main avenue some three-quarters of a mile, and then groups and couples began to slip aside into branch avenues, fly along the dismal corridors, and take each other by surprise at points where the corridors joined again. Parties were able to avoid each other for the space of half an hour without going beyond the "known" ground.

By and by, one group after another came straggling back to the mouth of the cave, panting, hilarious, smeared from head to foot with candle drippings, smeared with clay, and entirely delighted with the success of the day. Then they were astonished to find that they had been taking no note of time and that night was about at hand. The clanging bell had been calling for half an hour. However, this sort of close to the day's adventures was romantic and therefore satisfactory. When the ferry-boat with her wild freight pushed into the stream, nobody cared for the wasted time but the captain of the craft.

Remember that while Tom went off to the picnic, Huck decided to wait outside the local tavern to keep watch for Injun Joe and clues to find the treasure in hiding place Number Two. His wait is about to pay off!

Huck was already upon his watch when the ferry-boat's lights went glinting past the wharf. He heard no noise on board, for the young people were as subdued and still as people usually are who are nearly tired to death. He wondered what boat it was, and why she did not stop at the wharf—and then he dropped her out of his mind and put his attention upon his business. The night was growing cloudy and dark. Ten o'clock came, and the noise of vehicles ceased, scattered lights began to wink out, all straggling foot passengers disappeared and left the small watcher alone with the silence and the ghosts. Eleven o'clock came, and the tavern lights were put out; darkness everywhere, now. Huck waited what seemed a weary long time, but nothing happened. His faith was weakening. Was there really any use? Why not give it up and turn in?

A noise fell upon his ear. He was all attention in an instant. The alley door closed softly. He sprang to the corner of the brick store. The next moment two men brushed by him, and one seemed to have something under his arm. **I'll just bet that's Injun Joe—with the treasure!** It must be that box! So they were going to remove the treasure. Why call Tom now? It would be absurd—the men would get away with the box and never be found again. No, he would stick to their wake and follow them; he would trust to the darkness for security from discovery. Huck stepped out and glided along behind the men, cat-like, with bare feet, allowing them to keep just far enough ahead not to be invisible.

They moved up the river street three blocks, then turned to the left up a cross street. They went straight ahead, then, until they came to the path that led up Cardiff Hill; this they took. They passed by the old Welchman's house, half way up the hill without hesitating, and still climbed upward. **The old Welchman is a friend of Huck's. His name is Mr.**

Jones, and it's a good thing he's close by. Tracking Injun Joe is a dangerous business, and Huck might need help. Good, thought Huck, they will bury it in the stone pit. But they never stopped. They passed on, up the summit. They plunged into the narrow path between the tall sumach bushes, and were at once hidden in the gloom. Huck closed up and shortened his distance, now, for they would never be able to see him. He trotted along awhile; then slowed his pace, fearing he was gaining too fast; moved on a piece, then stopped altogether; listened; no sound; none, save the beating of his own heart. The hooting of an owl came from over the hill. But no footsteps. Heaven, was everything lost! He was about to spring with winged feet, when a man cleared his throat not four feet from him! Huck's heart shot into his throat, but he swallowed it again; and then he stood there shaking as if a dozen fevers had taken charge of him at once, and so weak that he thought he must surely fall to the ground. He knew where he was. He knew he was within five steps of the stile leading into Widow Douglas's grounds. Very well, he thought, let them bury it there; it won't be hard to find.

A STILE is a group of steps for getting over a fence or wall.

Now there was a voice—a very low voice—Injun Joe's.

"Damn her, maybe she's got company—there's lights, late as it is."

"I can't see any."

This was that stranger's voice—the stranger of the haunted house. A deadly chill went to Huck's heart—this, then, was the "revenge" job! His thought was, to fly. Then he remembered that the Widow Douglas had been kind to him more than once, and maybe these men were going to murder her. He wished he dared venture to warn her; but knew he didn't dare—they might come and catch him. He thought all this and more in the moment between the stranger's remark and Injun Joe's next—which was—

"Because the bush is in your way. Now—this way—now you see, don't you?"

"Yes. Well there *is* company there, I reckon. Better give it up."

"Give it up, and I just leaving this country forever! Give it up and maybe never have another chance. I tell you again, and I've told you before, her husband was rough on me—many times he was rough on me—and mainly he was the justice of the peace that jailed me for a vagrant. And that ain't all. It ain't a millionth part of it! He had me *horsewhipped*!—with all the town looking on! HORSEWHIPPED!—do you understand? He took advantage of me and died. But I'll take it out of *her*."

"Well, if it's got to be done, let's get at it. The quicker the better—I'm all in a shiver."

"Do it *now*? And company there? No—we'll wait till the lights are out—there's no hurry."

Huck felt that a silence was going to follow—a thing still more awful than any amount of murderous talk; so he held his breath and stepped gingerly back; planted his foot carefully and firmly, after balancing, one-legged, in a precarious way and almost toppling over, first on one side and then on the other. He took another step back, then another and another, and—a twig snapped under his foot! His breath stopped and he listened. There was no sound—the stillness was perfect. His gratitude was measureless. Now he turned in his tracks, between the walls of sumach bushes—turned himself as carefully as if he were a ship—and then stepped quickly but cautiously along. When he emerged at the stone pit he felt secure, and so he picked up his nimble heels and flew. Down, down he sped, till he reached the Welchman's. He banged at the door, and presently the heads of the old man and his two husky sons were thrust from windows.

"What's the row there? Who's banging? What do you want?"

"Let me in—quick! I'll tell everything."

"Why who are you?"

"Huckleberry Finn—quick, let me in!"

"Huckleberry Finn, indeed! It ain't a name to open many doors, I judge! But let him in, lads, and let's see what's the trouble."

"Please don't ever tell *I* told you," were Huck's first words when he got in. "Please don't—I'd be killed, sure—but the Widow's been good friends to me sometimes, and I want to tell—I *will* tell if you'll promise you won't ever say it was me."

"By George he *has* got something to tell, or he wouldn't act so!" exclaimed the old man; "out with it and nobody here'll ever tell, lad."

Three minutes later the old man and his sons, well armed, were up the hill, and just entering the sumach path on tip-toe, their weapons in their hands. Huck accompanied them no further. He hid behind a great bowlder and fell to listening. There was a lagging, anxious silence, and then all of a sudden there was an explosion of firearms and a cry.

Huck waited for no particulars. He sprang away and sped down the hill as fast as his legs could carry him.

17
The Story Circulated

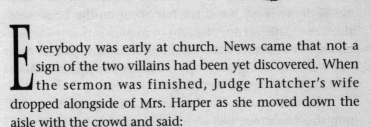

Now it's Huck's turn to be a hero! By going to the Welchman for help, Huck saved the life of the Widow Douglas. He told the Welchman of Injun Joe's plan, and old Mr. Jones and his sons went out to capture the villains. Injun Joe escaped, but the Widow Douglas is safe. Huck goes to see the Welchman the next day, but all the excitement has made him ill, and the Welchman puts Huck to bed to rest. Everyone in town is talking about the incident . . . until they realize another important event has occurred.

Everybody was early at church. News came that not a sign of the two villains had been yet discovered. When the sermon was finished, Judge Thatcher's wife dropped alongside of Mrs. Harper as she moved down the aisle with the crowd and said:

"Is my Becky going to sleep all day? I just expected she would be tired to death."

"Your Becky?"

"Yes," with a startled look—"didn't she stay with you last night?"

"Why, no."

Mrs. Thatcher turned pale, and sank into a pew, just as Aunt Polly, talking briskly with a friend, passed by. Aunt Polly said:

"Good morning, Mrs. Thatcher. Good morning, Mrs. Harper. I've got a boy that's turned up missing. I reckon my Tom staid at your house last night—one of you. And now he's afraid to come to church. I've got to settle with him."

Mrs. Thatcher shook her head feebly and turned paler than ever.

"He didn't stay with us," said Mrs. Harper, beginning to look uneasy. A marked anxiety came into Aunt Polly's face.

"Joe Harper, have you seen my Tom this morning?"

"No'm."

"When did you see him last?"

Joe tried to remember, but was not sure he could say. The people had stopped moving out of church. Whispers passed along, and an uneasiness took possession of every face. Children were anxiously questioned, and young teachers. They all said they had not noticed whether Tom and Becky were on board the ferry-boat on the homeward trip; it was dark; no one thought of inquiring if any one was missing. One young man finally blurted out his fear that they were still in the cave! Mrs. Thatcher fainted away. Aunt Polly fell to crying and wringing her hands.

The alarm swept from lip to lip, from group to group, from street to street, and within five minutes the bells were wildly clanging and the whole town was up! The Widow Douglas episode sank into instant insignificance, the burglars were forgotten, horses were saddled, skiffs were manned, the ferry-boat ordered out, and before the horror was half an hour old, two hundred men were pouring down high-road and river toward the cave.

The old Welchman came home toward daylight, spattered with candle grease, smeared with clay, and almost worn out. **The Welchman had been part of the group searching in the cave for Tom and Becky.** He found Huck still in the bed that had been provided for him, and delirious with fever. The physicians were all at the cave, so the Widow Douglas came and took charge of the patient. She said she would do her best by him, because, whether he was good, bad, or indifferent, he was the Lord's, and nothing that was the Lord's was a thing to be neglected.

18
Lost in the Cave

Are you wondering what happened to Becky and Tom in the cave? Now we are going to go back in time and find out.

Now to return to Tom and Becky's share in the picnic. They tripped along the murky aisles with the rest of the company, visiting the familiar wonders of the cave—wonders dubbed with rather over-descriptive names, such as "The Drawing-Room," "The Cathedral," "Aladdin's Palace," and so on. Presently the hide-and-seek frolicking began, and Tom and Becky engaged in it with zeal. Then they wandered down a twisting avenue holding their candles aloft and reading the tangled web-work of names, dates, post-office addresses and mottoes with which the rocky walls had been frescoed (in candle smoke). **Walls that are "frescoed" are painted. In this case, the cave walls are "painted" by using the smoke from their candles.** Still drifting along and talking, they scarcely noticed that they were now in a part of the cave whose walls were not frescoed. They smoked their own names under an overhanging shelf and moved on. Presently they came to a place where a little stream of water, trickling over a ledge and carrying a limestone sediment with it, had, in the slow-dragging ages, formed a Niagara in gleaming and imperishable stone. Tom squeezed his small body behind it in order to illuminate it for Becky. He found a steep natural stairway which was enclosed between narrow walls, and at once the ambition to be a discoverer seized him. Becky responded to his call, and they made a smoke-mark for future guidance, and started upon their quest. They wound this way and that, far down into the secret depths of the cave, made another mark, and branched off in search of novelties to tell the upper world about. In one place they found a spacious cavern, from whose ceiling depended a multitude of shining stalactites the length of a man's leg; they walked all about it, wondering and admiring, and presently left it by one of the numerous passages that opened into it. **Stalactites and stalagmites are mineral deposits in caves that look like long teeth. Stalactites hang down from the ceiling, and stalagmites poke up from the ground.** This shortly brought them to a bewitching spring, whose basin was covered with a frost work of glittering crystals; it was in the midst of a cavern whose walls were supported by many fantastic pillars which had been formed by the joining of great stalactites and stalagmites together, the result of the ceaseless water-drip of centuries. Under the roof vast knots of bats had packed themselves together, thousands in a bunch; the lights disturbed the creatures and they came flocking down by hundreds, squeaking and darting furiously at the candles. Tom knew their ways and the danger of this sort of conduct. He seized Becky's hand and hurried her into the first corridor that offered; and none too soon, for a bat struck Becky's light out with its wing

while she was passing out of the cavern. The bats chased the children a good distance; but the fugitives plunged into every new passage that offered, and at last got rid of the perilous things. Tom found an underground lake, shortly, which stretched its dim length away until its shape was lost in the shadows. He wanted to explore its borders, but concluded that it would be best to sit down and rest a while,

It would be terrifying to be chased by bats!

first. Now, for the first time, the deep stillness of the place laid a clammy hand upon the spirits of the children. Becky said:

"Why, I didn't notice, but it seems ever so long since I heard any of the others."

"Come to think, Becky, we are away down below them—and I don't know how far away north, or south, or east, or whichever it is. We couldn't hear them here."

Becky grew fearful.

"I wonder how long we've been down here, Tom. We better start back."

"Yes, I reckon we better. P'raps we better."

"Can you find the way, Tom? It's all a mixed-up crookedness to me."

"I reckon I could find it—but then the bats. If they put both our candles out it will be an awful fix. Let's try some other way, so as not to go through there."

"Well. But I hope we won't get lost. It would be so awful!" and the girl shuddered at the thought of the dreadful possibilities.

They started through a corridor, and traversed it in silence a long way, glancing at each new opening, to see if there was anything familiar about the look of it; but they were all strange. Every time Tom made an examination, Becky would watch his face for an encouraging sign, and he would say cheerily—

"Oh, it's all right. This ain't the one, but we'll come to it right away!"

But he felt less and less hopeful with each failure, and presently began to turn off into diverging avenues at sheer random, in desperate hope of finding the one that was wanted. **It's like being trapped in a giant maze. All of their twists**

117

and turns seem to lead nowhere! He still said it was "all right," but there was such a leaden dread at his heart, that the words had lost their ring and sounded just as if he had said, "All is lost!" Becky clung to his side in an anguish of fear, and tried hard to keep back the tears, but they would come. At last she said:

"O, Tom, never mind the bats, let's go back that way! We seem to get worse and worse off all the time."

Tom stopped.

"Listen!" said he.

Profound silence; silence so deep that even their breathings were obvious in the hush. Tom shouted. The call went echoing down the empty aisles and died out in the distance in a faint sound that resembled a ripple of mocking laughter.

"Oh, don't do it again, Tom, it is too horrid," said Becky.

"It is horrid, but I better, Becky; they might *hear* us, you know," and he shouted again.

The children stood still and listened; but there was no result. Tom turned upon the back track at once, and hurried his steps. It was but a little while before a certain indecision in his manner revealed another fearful fact to Becky—he could not find his way back! **Uh-oh. Before they were just mostly lost. Now they're completely lost!**

"O, Tom, you didn't make any marks!"

"Becky I was such a fool! Such a fool! I never thought we might want to come back! No—I can't find the way. It's all mixed up."

"Tom, Tom, we're lost! we're lost! We never can get out of this awful place! O, why *did* we ever leave the others!"

She sank to the ground and burst into such a frenzy of

crying that Tom was appalled with the idea that she might die, or loose her reason. He sat down by her and put his arms around her; she buried her face in his chest, she clung to him, she poured out her terrors, her unavailing regrets, and the far echoes turned them all to jeering laughter. Tom begged her to pluck up hope again, and she said she could not. He fell to blaming and abusing himself for getting her into this miserable situation; this had a better effect. She said she would try to hope again, she would get up and follow wherever he might lead if only he would not talk like that any more. For he was no more to blame than she, she said.

So they moved on, again—aimlessly—simply at random—all they could do was to move, keep moving. For a little while, hope made a show of reviving.

By and by Tom took Becky's candle and blew it out. This economy meant so much! Words were not needed. Becky understood, and her hope died again. She knew that Tom had a whole candle and three or four pieces in his pockets—yet he must economize.

To economize means to avoid waste. Since Tom and Becky only need one candle, Tom is economizing by saving Becky's candle.

By and by fatigue began to grow; the children tried to pay no attention, for it was dreadful to think of sitting down when time was so precious; moving, in some direction, in any direction, was at least progress and might bear fruit; but to sit down was to invite death.

At last Becky's frail limbs refused to carry her farther. She sat down. Tom rested with her, and they talked of home, and the friends there, and the comfortable beds and above all, the light! Becky cried, and Tom tried to think of some way of comforting her. Fatigue bore so heavily upon

Becky that she drowsed off to sleep. Tom was grateful. He sat looking into her drawn face and saw it grow smooth and natural under the influence of pleasant dreams; and by and by a smile dawned and rested there. The peaceful face reflected somewhat of peace and healing into his own spirit, and his thoughts wandered away to by-gone times and dreamy memories. While he was deep in his thoughts, Becky woke up with a breezy little laugh—but it was stricken dead upon her lips, and a groan followed it.

"Oh, how *could* I sleep! I wish I never, never had waked! No! No, I don't, Tom! Don't look so! I won't say it again."

"I'm glad you've slept, Becky; you'll feel rested, now, and we'll find the way out."

"We can try, Tom; but I've seen such a beautiful country in my dream. I reckon we are going there."

"Maybe not, maybe not. Cheer up, Becky, and let's go on trying."

They rose up and wandered along, hand in hand and hopeless. They tried to estimate how long they had been in the cave, but all they knew was that it seemed days and weeks, and yet it was plain that this could not be, for their candles were not gone yet. A long time after this—they could not tell how long—Tom said they must go softly and listen for dripping water—they must find a spring. They found one presently, and Tom said it was time to rest again. Both were cruelly tired, yet Becky said she thought she could go on a little farther. She was surprised to hear Tom disagree. She could not understand it. They sat down, and Tom fastened his candle to the wall in front of them with some clay. Nothing was said for some time. Then Becky broke the silence:

"Tom, I am so hungry!"

Tom took something out of his pocket.

"Do you remember this?" said he.

Becky almost smiled.

"It's our wedding cake, Tom."

"Yes—I wish it was as big as a barrel, for it's all we've got."

"I saved it from the picnic for us to dream on, Tom, the way grown up people do with wedding cake—but it'll be our—"

She dropped the sentence where it was. Tom divided the cake and Becky ate with good appetite, while Tom nibbled at his portion. There was abundance of cold water to finish the feast with. By and by Becky suggested that they move on again. Tom was silent a moment. Then he said:

"Becky, can you bear it if I tell you something?"

Becky's face paled, but she thought she could.

"Well then, Becky, we must stay here, where there's water to drink. That little piece is our last candle!"

Becky gave loose to tears and wailings. Tom did what he could to comfort her but with little effect. At length Becky said:

"Tom!"

"Well, Becky?"

"They'll miss us and hunt for us!"

"Yes, they will! Certainly they will!"

"Maybe they're hunting for us now, Tom."

"Why I reckon maybe they are. I hope they are."

"When would they miss us, Tom?"

"When they get back to the boat, I reckon."

"Tom, it might be dark, then—would they notice we hadn't come?"

"I don't know. But anyway, your mother would miss you as soon as they got home."

A frightened look in Becky's face brought Tom to his senses and he saw that he had made a blunder. Becky was not to have gone home that night! The children became silent and thoughtful. In a moment a new burst of grief from Becky showed Tom that the thing in his mind had struck hers also—that the Sabbath morning might be half spent before Mrs. Thatcher discovered that Becky was not at Mrs. Harper's.

The children fastened their eyes upon their bit of candle and watched it melt slowly and pitilessly away; saw the half inch of wick stand alone at last; saw the feeble flame rise and fall, climb the thin column of smoke, linger at its top a moment, and then—the horror of utter darkness reigned! **Utter darkness! How will Tom and Becky ever find their way out?**

The hours wasted away, and hunger came to torment the captives again. A portion of Tom's half of the cake was left; they divided and ate it. But they seemed hungrier than before. The poor morsel of food only whetted desire.

By and by Tom said:

"*Sh!* Did you hear that?"

Both held their breath and listened. There was a sound like the faintest, far-off shout. Instantly Tom answered it, and leading Becky by the hand, started groping down the corridor in its direction. Presently he listened again; again the sound was heard, and apparently a little nearer.

"It's them!" said Tom; "they're coming! Come along Becky—we're all right now!"

The joy of the prisoners was almost overwhelming. Their speed was slow, however, because pitfalls were somewhat common, and had to be guarded against. They shortly came to one and had to stop. It might be three feet deep, it might be a hundred—there was no passing it at any rate. Tom got down on his breast and reached as far down as he could. No bottom. They must stay there and wait until the searchers came. They listened; evidently the distant shoutings were growing more distant! a moment or two more and they had gone altogether. The heart-sinking misery of it! Tom whooped until he was hoarse, but it was of no use. He talked hopefully to Becky; but an age of anxious waiting passed and no sounds came again.

The children groped their way back to the spring. The weary time dragged on; they slept again, and awoke starving and miserable. Tom believed it must be Tuesday by this time. **Remember that Tom and Becky entered the cave on Saturday. By his calculations, they've been lost underground for three days!**

Now an idea struck him. There were some side passages near at hand. It would be better to explore some of these than bear the weight of the heavy time in doing nothing. He took a kite-line from his pocket, tied it to a projection, and he and Becky started, Tom in the lead, unwinding the line as he groped along. At the end of twenty steps the corridor ended in a "jumping-off place." Tom got down on his knees and felt below, and then as far around the corner as he could reach with his hands conveniently; he made an effort to stretch yet a little further to the right, and at that moment, not twenty yards away, a human hand, holding a candle, appeared from behind a rock! Tom lifted up a glorious shout, and instantly that hand was followed by the body it belonged to—Injun Joe's! Tom could not move. He was vastly gratified the next moment, to see the villain take to his heels and get himself out of sight. **Injun Joe, here? What could he possibly be doing in the cave? More importantly, will he come after Tom?** Tom wondered that Joe had not recognized his voice and come over and killed him for testifying in court. But the echoes must have disguised the voice. Without doubt, that was it, he reasoned. Tom's fright weakened every muscle in his body. He said to himself that if he had strength enough to get back to the spring he would stay there, and nothing should tempt him to run the risk of meeting Injun Joe again. He was careful to keep from Becky what it was he had seen. He told her he had only shouted "for luck."

Whew! Only Tom saw Injun Joe. Becky has enough to worry about!

But hunger and wretchedness rise superior to fears in the long run. Another long and boring wait at the spring and another long sleep brought changes. The children awoke tortured with a raging hunger. Tom believed that it must be Wednesday or Thursday or even Friday or Saturday, now, and that the search had been given over. He proposed to explore another passage. He felt willing to risk Injun Joe and all other terrors. But Becky was very weak. She had sunk into a dreary apathy and would not be awakened. She said she would wait, now, where she was, and die—it would not be long. She told Tom to go with the kite-line and explore it if he chose; but she implored him to come back every little while and speak to her; and she made him promise that when the awful time came, he would stay by her and hold her hand until all was over.

Tom kissed her, with a choking sensation in his throat, and made a show of being confident of finding the searchers or an escape from the cave; then he took the kite-line in his hand and went groping down one of the passages on his hands and knees, distressed with hunger and sick with bodings of coming doom.

So Tom and Becky are still lost in the cave, in the dark, with no food. To make matters worse, Injun Joe is prowling around in the same cave! What if he finds the kids before they find a way out? The suspense is incredible—quick, turn the page!

19
Tom's Enemy in Safe Quarters

Tuesday afternoon came, and waned to the twilight. The village of St. Petersburg still mourned. The lost children had not been found. The village went to its rest on Tuesday night, sad and forlorn.

Away in the middle of the night a wild peal burst from the village bells, and in a moment the streets were swarming with frantic half-clad people, who shouted, "Turn out! turn out! they're found! they're found!" Tin pans and horns were added to the din, the population massed itself and moved toward the river, met the children coming in an open carriage drawn by shouting citizens, thronged around it, joined its homeward march, and swept magnificently up the main street roaring huzzah after huzzah!

The village was illuminated; nobody went to bed again; it was the greatest night the little town had ever seen. During the first half hour a procession of villagers filed through Judge Thatcher's house, seized the saved ones and kissed them, squeezed Mrs. Thatcher's hand, tried to speak but couldn't—and drifted out raining tears all over the place.

Aunt Polly's happiness was complete. Tom lay upon a sofa with an eager audience about him and told the history of the wonderful adventure, putting in many striking additions; and closed with a description of how he left

Becky and went on an exploring expedition; how he followed two avenues as far as his kite-line would reach; how he followed a third to the fullest stretch of the kite-line, and was about to turn back when he glimpsed a far-off speck that looked like daylight; dropped the line and groped toward it, pushed his head and shoulders through a small hole and saw the broad Mississippi rolling by! And if it had only happened to be night he would not have seen that speck of daylight and would not have explored that passage any more! He told how he went back for Becky and broke the good news and she told him not to fret her with such stuff, for she was tired, and knew she was going to die, and wanted to. He described how he labored with her and convinced her; and how she almost died for joy when she had groped to where she actually saw the blue speck of daylight; how he pushed his way out at the hole and then helped her out; how they sat there and cried for gladness; how some men came along in a skiff and Tom hailed them and told them their situation and their starved condition; how the men didn't believe the wild tale at first, "because," said they, "you are five miles down the river below the valley the cave is in"—then took them aboard, rowed to a house, gave them supper, made them rest till two or three hours after dark and then brought them home.

About two weeks after Tom's rescue from the cave, he started off to visit Huck, who had grown plenty strong enough, now, to hear exciting talk, and Tom had some that would interest him, he thought. Judge Thatcher's house was on Tom's way, and he stopped to see Becky. The judge and some friends set Tom to talking, and some one asked him if he wouldn't like to go to the cave again. Tom said he thought he wouldn't mind it. The judge said:

"Well, there are others just like you, Tom, I've not the least doubt. But we have taken care of that. Nobody will get lost in that cave any more."

"Why?"

"Because I had its big door sheathed with boiler iron two weeks ago, and triple-locked—and I've got the keys."

Tom turned white as a sheet.

"What's the matter boy? Here, run somebody! Fetch a glass of water!"

The water was brought and thrown into Tom's face.

"Ah, now you're all right. What was the matter with you, Tom?"

"Oh, Judge, Injun Joe's in the cave!"

That's right! With all this excitement, I almost forgot about Injun Joe. But if Injun Joe was in the cave when it was sealed up tight . . . and if he didn't have any way out . . . yikes!

20

An Expedition
to the Cave

Within a few minutes the news had spread, and a dozen skiff-loads of men were on their way to McDougal's cave, and the ferry-boat, well filled with passengers, soon followed. Tom Sawyer was in the skiff that bore Judge Thatcher.

When the cave door was unlocked, a sorrowful sight presented itself in the dim twilight of the place. Injun Joe lay stretched upon the ground, dead, with his face close to the crack of the door, as if his longing eyes had been fixed, to the latest moment, upon the light and the cheer of the free world outside. Tom was touched, for he knew by his own experience how this wretch had suffered. His pity was moved, but nevertheless he felt an abounding sense of relief and security, now.

Injun Joe was buried near the mouth of the cave; and people flocked there in boats and wagons from the towns and from all the farms and hamlets for seven miles around; they brought their children, and all sorts of provisions, and confessed that they had had almost as satisfactory a time at the funeral as they could have had at the hanging.

The morning after the funeral Tom took Huck to a private place to have an important talk. Huck had learned all about Tom's adventure from the Welchman and the

Widow Douglas, by this time, but Tom said he reckoned there was one thing they had not told him; that thing was what he wanted to talk about now.

Huck searched his comrade's face keenly. "Tom, have you got on the track of that money again?"

"Huck, it's in the cave!"

Huck's eyes blazed.

"Say it again, Tom!"

"The money's in the cave!"

"Tom—honest injun, now—is it fun, or earnest?"

"Earnest, Huck—just as earnest as ever I was in my life. Will you go in there with me and help get it out?"

"I bet I will! I will if it's where we can blaze our way to it and not get lost."

"Huck, we can do that without the least little bit of trouble in the world."

"Good as wheat! What makes you think the money's—"

"Huck, you just wait till we get in there. If we don't find it I'll agree to give you my drum and everything I've got in the world. I will, by jingo."

"All right—it's a whiz. When do you say?"

"Right now, if you say it. Are you strong enough?"

"Is it far in the cave? I ben on my pins a little, three or four days, now, but I can't walk more'n a mile, Tom—least I don't think I could."

Huck is calling his legs "pins." He has been so ill, he only starting walking three or four days ago.

"It's about five mile into there the way anybody but me would go, Huck, but there's a mighty short cut that don't anybody but me know about. Huck, I'll take you right to it in a skiff. I'll float the skiff down there, and I'll pull it back again all by myself. You needn't ever turn your hand over."

"Less start right off, Tom."

"All right. We want some bread and meat and our pipes, and a little bag or two, and two or three kite-strings, and some of these new fangled things they call lucifer matches. I tell you many's the time I wished I had some when I was in there before." **Back then, matches were still a new invention.**

A trifle after noon the boys borrowed a small skiff and got under way at once. When they were several miles below "Cave Hollow," Tom said:

"Now you see this bluff here looks all alike all the way down from the cave hollow—no houses, no wood-yards, bushes all alike. But do you see that white place up yonder where there's been a land-slide? Well that's one of my marks. We'll get ashore, now."

They landed.

"Now Huck, where we're a-standing you could touch that hole I got out of. See if you can find it."

Huck searched all the place about, and found nothing. Tom proudly marched into a thick clump of sumach bushes and said—

"Here you are! Look at it, Huck; it's the snuggest hole in this country. You just keep mum about it. All along I've been wanting to be a robber, but I knew I'd got to have a place like this, and where to run across it was the bother. We've got it now, and we'll keep it quiet, only we'll let Joe Harper and Ben Rogers in—because of course there's got to be a Gang, or else there wouldn't be any style about it. Tom Sawyer's Gang—it sounds splendid, don't it Huck?"

"Well, it just does, Tom.

The boys entered the hole, Tom in the lead. They toiled their way to the farther end of the tunnel, then made their spliced kite-strings fast and moved on. Tom whispered—

"Now I'll show you something, Huck."

He held his candle aloft and said—

"Look as far around the corner as you can. Do you see that? There—on the big rock over yonder—done with candle smoke."

"Tom, it's a *cross*!"

"*Now* where's your Number Two? '*Under the cross,*' hey? Right yonder's where I saw Injun Joe poke up his candle, Huck!"

Huck stared at the mystic sign a while, and then said with a shaky voice—

"Tom, less git out of here!"

"What! and leave the treasure?"

"Yes—leave it. Injun Joe's ghost is round about there, certain."

"No, it ain't, Huck, no it ain't. It would ha'nt the place where he died—away out at the mouth of the cave—five mile from here."

"No, Tom, it wouldn't. It would hang round the money. I know the ways of ghosts, and so do you."

Tom began to fear that Huck was right. Misgivings gathered in his mind. But presently an idea occurred to him—

"Looky here, Huck, what fools we're making of ourselves! Injun Joe's ghost ain't a going to come around where there's a cross!"

The point was well taken. It had its effect.

"Tom I didn't think of that. But that's so. It's luck for us, that cross is. I reckon we'll climb down there and have a hunt for that box."

Tom went first, cutting rude steps in the clay hill as he descended. Huck followed. Four avenues opened out of the small cavern which the great rock stood in. The boys examined three of them with no result. They found a small recess in the one nearest the base of the rock, with a pallet of blankets spread down in it; also an old suspender, some bacon rhind, and the well gnawed bones of two or three fowls. But there was no money box. The lads searched and re-searched this place, but in vain. Tom said:

"He said *under* the cross. Well, this comes nearest to being under the cross. It can't be under the rock itself, because that sets solid on the ground."

They searched everywhere once more, and then sat down discouraged. Huck could suggest nothing. By and by Tom said:

"Looky here, Huck, there's footprints and some candle grease on the clay about one side of this rock, but not on the other sides. Now what's that for? I bet you the money *is* under the rock. I'm going to dig in the clay."

"That ain't no bad notion, Tom!" said Huck with animation.

Tom's "real Barlow" was out at once, and he had not dug four inches before he struck wood.

The "real Barlow" is a knife, and Tom is using it for more digging! I bet now they REALLY wish they had a canine digging expert to help them.

"Hey, Huck!—you hear that?"

Huck began to dig and scratch now. Some boards were soon uncovered and removed. They had concealed a natural opening which led under the rock. Tom got into this and held his candle as far under the rock as he could, but said he could not see to the end. He proposed to explore. He stooped and passed under; the narrow way descended gradually. He followed its winding course, first to the right, then to the left, Huck at his heels. Tom turned a short curve, by and by, and exclaimed—

"My goodness, Huck, looky here!"

It was a treasure box, sure enough, occupying a snug little cavern, along with an empty powder keg, a couple of guns in leather cases, two or three pairs of old moccasins, a leather belt, and some other rubbish well soaked with the water-drip.

"Got it at last!" said Huck, plowing among the tarnished coins with his hand. "My, but we're rich, Tom!"

21
New Adventures Planned

Tom and Huck returned to town heroes again — and wealthy ones at that! Widow Douglas throws a party to thank Huck for saving her life. She announces that she wants to give Huck a proper home and is adopting him.

The reader may rest satisfied that Tom's and Huck's windfall made a mighty stir in the poor little village of St. Petersburg. So vast a sum, all in actual cash, seemed next to incredible. It was talked about, gloated over, glorified, until the reason of many of the citizens tottered under the strain of the unhealthy excitement. Every "haunted" house in St. Petersburg and the neighboring villages was dissected, plank by plank, and its foundations dug up and ransacked for hidden treasure—and not by boys, but men. Wherever Tom and Huck appeared they were courted, admired, stared at. Now their sayings were treasured and repeated; everything they did seemed somehow to be regarded as remarkable; they had evidently lost the power of doing and saying commonplace things. The village paper published biographical sketches of the boys.

Each lad had an income, now, that was simply huge—a dollar for every weekday in the year and half of the Sundays. A dollar and a quarter a week would board, lodge and school a boy in those old simple days—and clothe him and wash him, too, for that matter.

Judge Thatcher had a great opinion of Tom. He said that no common-place boy would ever have got his daughter out of the cave.

Judge Thatcher hoped to see Tom a great lawyer or a great soldier some day. He said he meant to look to it that Tom should be admitted to the National Military academy and afterward trained in the best law school in the country, in order that he might be ready for either career or both.

Huck Finn's wealth and the fact that he was now under the Widow Douglas's protection, introduced him into society—no, dragged him into it, hurled him into it—and his sufferings were almost more than he could bear. The widow's servants kept him clean and neat, combed and brushed, and they bedded him nightly in unsympathetic sheets that had not one little spot or stain which he could press to his heart and know for a friend. He had to eat with knife and fork; he had to use napkin, cup and plate; he had to learn his book, he had to go to church; he had to talk so properly that speech was become tasteless in his mouth; withersoever he turned, the bars and chains of civilization shut him in and bound him hand and foot.

He bravely bore his miseries three weeks, and then one day turned up missing. For forty-eight hours the widow hunted for him everywhere in great distress. The public were profoundly concerned; they searched high and low, they dragged the river for his body. Early the third morning Tom Sawyer wisely went poking among some old empty hogsheads down behind the abandoned slaughterhouse, and in one of them he found the refugee. Huck had slept there; he had just breakfasted upon some stolen odds and ends of food, and was lying off, now, in comfort with his pipe. He was unkempt, uncombed, and clad in the same old ruin of rags that had made him picturesque in the days when he was free and happy. Tom dug him out, told him the trouble he had been causing, and urged him to go home. Huck's face lost its tranquil content. He said:

"Don't talk about it, Tom. I've tried it, and it don't work; it don't work, Tom. It ain't for me; I ain't used to it. The widder's good to me, and friendly; but I can't stand them ways. She makes me git up just at the same time every morning; she makes me wash, they comb me all to thunder; she won't let me sleep in the wood-shed; I got to wear them blamed clothes that just smothers me, Tom; they don't seem to any air git through 'em, somehow; and they're so rotten nice that I can't set down, nor lay down, nor roll around anywher's; I hain't slid on a cellar-door for—well, it 'pears to be years; I got to go to church and sweat and sweat—I hate them ornery sermons! I can't ketch a fly in there, I can't chaw, I got to wear shoes all Sunday. The widder eats by a bell; she goes to bed by a bell; she gits up by a bell—everything's so awful reg'lar a body can't stand it"

"Well, everybody does that way, Huck."

"Tom, it don't make no difference. I ain't everybody, and I can't *stand* it. It's awful to be tied up so. And grub comes too easy—I don't take no interest in vittles, that way. I got to ask, to go a-fishing; I got to ask, to go in a-swimming—dern'd if I hain't got to ask to do everything. Well, I'd got to talk so nice it wasn't no comfort—I'd got to go up in the attic and rip out a while, every day, to git a

137

taste in my mouth, or I'd a died, Tom. The widder wouldn't let me smoke; she wouldn't let me yell, she wouldn't let me gape, nor stretch, nor scratch, before folks—and dad fetch it, she prayed all the time! I never *see* such a woman! I *had* to shove, Tom—I just had to. And besides, that school's going to open, and I'd a had to go to it—well, I wouldn't stand *that* Tom. Lookyhere, Tom, being rich ain't what it's cracked up to be. It's just worry and worry, and sweat and sweat, and a-wishing you was dead all the time. Now these clothes suits me, and this barrel suits me, and I ain't ever going to shake 'em any more. Tom, I wouldn't ever got into all this trouble if it hadn't 'a' been for that money; now you just take my sheer of it along with your'n, and gimme a ten-center sometimes— not many times."

"Oh, Huck, you know I can't do that. 'Taint fair; and besides if you'll try this thing just a while longer you'll come to like it."

"Like it! Yes—the way I'd like a hot stove if I was to set on it long enough. No, Tom, I won't be rich, and I won't live in them cussed smothery houses. I like the woods, and the river, and hogsheads, and I'll stick to 'em, too. Blame it all! just as we'd got guns, and a cave, and all just fixed to rob, here this dern foolishness had got to come up and spile it all!"

Tom saw his opportunity —

"Lookyhere, Huck, being rich ain't going to keep me back from turning robber."

"No! Oh, good-licks, are you in real dead-wood earnest, Tom?"

"Just as dead earnest as I'm a sitting here. But Huck, we can't let you into the gang if you ain't respectable, you know."

Huck's joy was quenched.

"Can't let me in, Tom? Didn't you let me go for a pirate?"

"Yes, but that's different. A robber is more high-toned than what a pirate is—as a general thing. In most countries they're awful high up in the nobility—dukes and such."

"Now Tom, hain't you always ben friendly to me? You wouldn't shet me out, would you, Tom? You wouldn't do that, now, *would* you, Tom?"

"Huck, I wouldn't want to, and I *don't* want to—but what would people say? Why they'd say, 'Mph! Tom Sawyer's Gang! pretty low characters in it!' They'd mean you, Huck. You wouldn't like that, and I wouldn't."

Huck was silent for some time, engaged in a mental struggle. Finally he said:

"Well, I'll go back to the widder for a month and tackle it and see if I can come to stand it, if you'll let me b'long to the gang, Tom."

"All right, Huck, it's a whiz! Come along, old chap, and I'll ask the widow to let up on you a little, Huck."

"Will you Tom—now will you? That's good. If she'll let up on some of the roughest things, I'll smoke private and cuss private. When you going to start the gang and turn robbers?"

"Oh, right off. We'll get the boys together and have the initiation tonight, maybe."

"Have the which?"

"Have the initiation."

"What's that?"

"It's to swear to stand by one another, and never tell the gang's secrets, even if you're chopped all to flinders, and kill anybody and all his family that hurts one of the gang."

"That's great, Tom, I tell you."

"Well I bet it is. And all that swearing's got to be done at midnight, in the lonesomest, awfulest place you can find—a ha'nted house is the best, but they're all ripped up now."

"Well, midnight's good, anyway, Tom."

"Yes, so it is. And you've got to swear on a coffin, and sign it with blood."

"Now that's something *like*! Why it's a million times bullier than pirating. I'll stick to the widder till I rot, Tom; and if I git to be a reg'lar ripper of a robber, and everybody talking 'bout it, I reckon she'll be proud she dragged me in out of the wet."

And so this particular adventure of our two heroes draws to a close. But it's not the end, really. Mark Twain wrote about Tom and Huck in another great book called THE ADVENTURES OF HUCKLEBERRY FINN. That book is also full of adventure and excitement. Hey, all this excitement has got this little dog hungry. It's snack time, and I AM OUTTA HERE! See ya!

GLOSSARY

averted — turned away

eloquent — expressive; persuasive; clearly understood

furtive — on the sly; without being noticed

illuminate — to light up

inspiration — idea

manifest — become obvious; become clear

ruffian — cruel; tough person

stolid — showing no emotion

sumptuously — magnificently; grand; rich

vagrant — someone or something that moves from place to place without a definite course

vanity — pride

vise — clamp used to hold an object